MURDER MOST ILLEGAL

A CAROLYN NEVILLE MYSTERY BOOK 6

JOHN DUCKWORTH

Murder Most Illegal
Paperback Edition

CKN Christian Publishing
An Imprint of Wolfpack Publishing
5130 S. Fort Apache Rd. 215-380
Las Vegas, NV 89148

www.christiankindlenews.com

This book is a work of fiction. Any references to historical events, real people or real places are used fictitiously. Other names, characters, places and events are products of the author's imagination, and any resemblance to actual events, places or persons, living or dead, is entirely coincidental.

eBook ISBN 978-1-64734-538-9
Paperback ISBN 978-1-64734-539-6

To my brothers, Paul and Mark,
without whom I would be an only child.

MURDER MOST ILLEGAL

PROLOGUE

"HUNTER'S JUST *WEIRD*," STEPHEN SAID AS WE HEADED toward our cars.

"Just noticed?" I asked, fishing keys from my purse.

"Oh, crap," Stephen said. "Some kind of accident."

I glanced up. Two squad cars, lights flashing. Four cops directing traffic. Two drivers talking on cellphones. A garbage truck with a Yellow taxi scrunched under it, looking ready to be hauled away.

We didn't need a KFRC radio traffic report to tell us we needed a different route.

"Cut through the alley," I said.

Wending our way through the honks and expletives, we ducked between filthy brick walls and tried to get oriented.

"We're two blocks west," Stephen said.

"Three blocks east."

He took out his phone.

"It doesn't know where we parked," I said. "Let's just follow our instincts. We'll start with mine."

We picked our way past a dumpster and an uncapped

50-gallon drum a Greek restaurant was using to collect grease. It smelled like orange peels and rancid saganaki cheese.

I coughed. "Now, if you look past that wino and to the right—"

Suddenly I heard footsteps behind me.

"Hold it," said a voice. Whirling, I faced a figure in black sweatsuit and matching bandana mask. Sounded like a woman, but I couldn't be sure. The slender, flat-chested physique provided no gender reveal.

"You know," he or she said, "you really ought to let the cops and lawyers handle the legal stuff."

I looked down at my hand. Still holding my keys. Weren't you supposed to use them as weapons at times like these? The pepper spray was unreachable, but—

"Is this a mugging, or what?" Stephen asked, sounding impatient.

"A warning," said our assailant.

"Where's your gun?"

"At home in a safe. I've got this." The androgynous ninja drew some kind of knife from its belt.

"Cool dagger."

"Not what it's called, but no matter. You getting my message?"

CHAPTER 1

NEVER GO OUT WITH A LAWYER, ESPECIALLY IF HE LOOKS like Robert Redford used to.

When the waiter at Ocean Prime on Manhattan's 57th Street came to take our order, he raised an eyebrow and a pencil. "May I have your autograph?"

Roger Trumbull smiled that crinkly smile. "Thanks, but I'm not him."

The server sighed. "Then would you like to hear our specials?"

"Sure."

He rattled them off, then dashed away to get our drinks. Roger studied the menu. "Want to share a Garlic Butter Seafood Boil?"

"I never want to smell like that on a first date."

"It's our second."

I felt my cheeks redden. My problem wasn't memory loss, but the memory of a guy who'd dumped me. Ancient history.

The server was back, setting two glasses of water with lemon in front of us. "Ready?"

Roger put the menu down. "No. I want to gaze into this lady's eyes for a few minutes."

"You have my permission." No, that didn't sound right. But the fact was it *felt* like a first date, at least in terms of Romantic Aspiration Perspiration.

Taking a second look at Roger, the young man seemed ready to ask for a driver's license to prove his guest had never starred in *Barefoot in the Park*. "Take all the time you need," he said, and left.

Roger folded his hands midway between napkin and silverware. "First time we went out, we talked office politics. And whether someone like yourself from Editorial could get along with someone like me from the Legal Department."

I sipped my lemon water. "Obviously impossible. But we could give it one more try."

"Tell me more about yourself," he said. "Ever married?"

I shook my head. "Engaged. Then disengaged."

"The guy must have been an idiot."

"Depends on what you mean by 'idiot'. I'm sure he'd disagree."

He took a long drink. "Hope this line of questioning doesn't make you uncomfortable."

"Not a bit." I smiled but felt like I was screaming in the vacuum of space because there was a hole in my astronaut suit. If I kept saying the wrong thing, I might never have a chance at a Meaningful Relationship again.

He lowered his head. "Didn't mean to—"

"My turn. *You* ever married?"

He looked away. "Yeah. Her name was Shari. High school sweetheart. Speech therapist. Died of ovarian cancer three years ago."

Not knowing what to say, I took a drink and nearly swallowed an ice cube. "Sorry," I said, and coughed.

"I have a grown daughter in Rhode Island. Married, no kids. She and her husband run a little art gallery. Mostly his stuff. Huge paintings of lobsters. And sea cucumbers."

The server returned, pencil poised above his pad. "What can I get you?"

"Lobster," I said. "And a house salad. Vinaigrette on the side."

Roger squinted at the menu. "Same for me, but substitute trout for the lobster and a big pile of wild rice. And no bones, okay?"

"We'll do our best." The waiter disappeared into the kitchen.

"I hate bones," Roger said.

We sat there for a moment, staring at our hands. Finally I cracked my knuckles, a bad habit I'd picked up from my father, but he was from Idaho.

"Not to change the subject, but what's it like to run the Legal Department?"

"Oh, has its moments. I get more of a kick out of doing *pro bono* cases." He grinned. "Makes me sound like a storefront lawyer with a shaggy perm and bell bottoms, doesn't it?"

"Or *The Equalizer*."

"If I had my way, I'd give Pendleton House the heave-ho and concentrate on death row inmates. But then I wouldn't be able to afford my Maserati." He looked up. "It's used, you know. But lovingly maintained."

When our food came, I declined the lobster bib. I'd been avoiding bibs since early childhood, having watched my older cousins wear them at the annual Door County Fish Boil in Wisconsin, where we almost always vacationed. They'd lost their interest in dignity sometime before I was born.

Things went well until Roger hit a bone in the trout. After prying it from his teeth with his thumbnail, he looked at it. "Could have choked. Ought to sue, but I guess I'll let it go."

By the time we finished dessert—chocolate mousse for him, tiramisu for me—we'd covered his hope for a grandchild and mine for a new boss. He was about to signal the waiter for the check when a young blonde lady wearing a tight gold blouse with a plunging neckline showed up at our table. A twinge of jealousy surprised me from behind.

"Would you mind signing my backside?" she asked, giggling.

"Pardon me?"

"The back of my blouse." She put a Sharpie on the table and turned around.

"You know, I'm not Robert Redford."

She turned back. "Well, of course not. You're the guy from the article in the *New York Post.* One of the city's most eligible lawyers, right? Forgot your name."

"Perry Mason."

"Right." She turned around. Shrugging, he wrote the name between her shoulder blades.

For the next hour or so we talked about subjects I hadn't addressed with a guy for years. Like cotton candy and fear of commitment. By the time we were done, I couldn't wait to hear the words *I'll call you* again.

The server handed me a box to hold the remaining half of my lobster. People from Idaho can make soup out of anything. At least my mother can. My dad will eat anything, so it works out perfectly.

When we got back to his car, I examined it with new

eyes. I'd heard of Maseratis but had never seen one in person. I ran my finger along the dark blue passenger side, which was reflective as a mirror under the parking lot lights.

"Oh, *crap!*" Roger blurted. "Somebody's keyed it."

I walked around to his side, bent down, and saw a five-foot scratch from rear fender to front door handle.

As if comforting his dearest friend, he placed a palm on the roof. "Not the first time. Cars like this draw vandals like flypaper. Or it could be some lowlife I 'equalized'." He gave me a smile. "Ignore it. I've got a tab going at Maaco."

Climbing into the car, he turned the key and adjusted the rearview mirror. "Really, it's fine. Can I call you again?"

I pretended to ponder it. Couldn't look too eager.

"At your earliest convenience," I said. "The earlier the better."

* * *

"Be with you in a minute."

My boss, Hunter Thicke, had his back to us. Squaring his shoulders, he wielded a golf club. The artificial turf under his shiny brown Oxfords was natural as his brushed-back black undercut.

"Silence in the gallery, please." Taking his stance, he aimed for a four-foot hole-in-one. Somehow, he managed to miss.

With a grunt he turned around. "You're probably wondering why I've called you here."

I elbowed the cinnamon-haired millennial at my side. Stephen Ames, my senior editor, flinched. "Well, *I'm* dying to know," I said.

Someone else came through the door. Gina Casebeer. Pendleton House's sharpest lawyer as far as I was concerned. The latest addition to her collection of glasses—red Pierre Cardin, I guessed—was perched atop her gray bangs. The specs were the only accessories I'd ever seen her wear, including the time she'd rescued me from the Seattle County Jail. I owed her a favor.

As usual she looked tired, like someone from the cast of *It's a Wonderful Life*—perhaps one of the townspeople who'd lost her money at the bank.

"Ah, Gina," Hunter said, leaning on his putter. "Thank you for coming. You look radiant."

"My batteries expire next week," she deadpanned.

"Gina's discovered a legal problem with one of our upcoming releases," he said. "Feel free to sit down." We all did.

She cleared her throat and took a legal pad from her purse. "To start with, a—"

Hunter held up his hand. "No offense, but I'll handle this. The title is *Lies and Whispers* by Kathleen Rosenthal. The singer."

"Broadway actress," I said.

"Ooh," said Stephen. "I read the manuscript. Makes the *National Enquirer* look like *The New Yorker.* And she names *names*."

Hunter nodded. "The most important of which is her ex-husband, Jason."

"Joey," Gina corrected.

"Not important. Kathleen claims he stole all her money, was unfaithful, and electrocuted the cat."

Stephen held up his hand like a school crossing guard. "No, she said—"

"Not only that," Hunter added. "Damaged her hearing with round-the-clock trombone playing."

I leaned forward. "*Drumming*. I read it too." If Hunter had flipped through any of our books, it didn't show.

"Anyway, he's suing us for alienation of affection, trademark violation, slander, and defamation of character."

Gina sighed. "Actually, it's defamation and *libel*. The allegations can't be proven, and the man has engaged an excellent law firm. Halyard, Lemmon, and Scott. We have to verify the story from other sources, or—"

"The book will be cancelled," Hunter said.

"Costly decision," I said. "One you'd like to avoid, I'm sure."

He picked up his putter again and pointed the grip at me. "You've got two weeks to fix it."

"How?"

"Do that thing you do."

"What thing?"

"All the so-called investigating. Clear this book and I won't fire you." He tapped Stephen's knee with the club's business end. "You, too." He smiled his Ted Bundy smile.

I looked at Gina. She was sliding her legal pad back in her purse.

"This law firm," I said. "Exactly how good are they?"

She put her glasses back down on her nose. "Heard of Gerry Spence?"

"Yeah. Never lost a criminal case in a trial by jury."

"Neither has Halyard, Lemmon, and Scott."

* * *

Back in my office, Stephen and I sat down. Rummaging through my top desk drawer for some Skinny Cow chocolate was a disappointment. All I could find was a box of wintergreen Tic Tacs, nearly empty. I offered one to Stephen.

"Don't care for my breath, is that it?"

I popped one in my mouth. "I'd rather not get close enough to know one way or the other."

He threw up his hands. "As aggressive as Gerry Spence?"

"We need help. Obviously won't get it from Our Friends in Legal."

I took the last mint and dropped the box in the wastebasket.

"I wonder," he said.

"Gina didn't seem to think so."

"Maybe Roger would see it differently."

I picked up the phone and got his secretary, Peggy Van Plugh. She sounded rushed, as if she'd been scaling a mountain of author consent forms.

"Is Roger there?"

"Who wants to know?"

"Carolyn Neville. Editorial."

Long pause. She went from harassed to icy in about 17 seconds. "Oh, I know you. Roger's latest office romance."

"I wouldn't call it—"

"I'm sure you wouldn't. Hold on."

I closed my eyes. The grapevine was alive and well, and my reputation was withering on it like a raisin.

Roger came on the line. "Carolyn? Peggy said you wanted to talk to me." If he was busy, he didn't sound like it. I could tell he was smiling.

"I've got a little problem."

"How can I help?"

"We've got fourteen days to vet *Lies and Whispers*."

"That's a toughie. What do you want?"

"Advice."

"For free?"

"Hey, you said you loved to work *pro bono*. And this is all about justice. For me."

He chuckled. "How about we discuss it this evening? Right after work."

"Where?"

"My office. We can get takeout if you want."

"Can I bring my senior editor?"

There was a pause. "Okay." I could tell it wasn't his first choice.

"Thanks."

"See you then." He hung up.

Stephen put his hands behind his head. "What kind of takeout?"

"Don't know."

"Hope I won't cramp your style. I hate being a third wheel."

"This is business, not pleasure."

"In this case it's hard to tell the difference."

"What do we pay you for? Don't you have something to do?"

He got up. "Maybe I should reread *Lies and Whispers*. Just the naughty bits, of course." He sauntered out, hands in his pockets.

That evening, after the imaginary whistle blew, I took my purse and stopped by Stephen's cubicle. He was reading, but not the book.

He looked up from his smartphone. "Searching for private detectives. In case we come up dry."

"Company won't spring for that. Not yet anyway."

"Fine." He put his phone in his pocket. "Does your boyfriend like Sichuan?"

"He's not my boyfriend, and I don't know."

"I'd settle for Mandarin if necessary."

I resisted the urge to hit him with my purse. "Let's go."

Peggy Van Plugh was gone by the time we got to Roger's office. A little surprising. She seemed like the type who'd work late.

The door was shut. I knocked. No response.

"Roger?"

"Maybe he's getting the food," Stephen said.

I opened the door. It whispered over the thick carpet.

He was at his desk. He seemed to be studying a leather-bound casebook the size of a sheet cake.

"We're here," I said.

He didn't move.

I stepped closer, then drew a quick breath.

Dropping my purse, I put my hand on the desk to steady myself.

Lightheaded, I felt his neck for a pulse. Nothing.

Slowly he fell forward, his expressionless face coming to rest squarely on the legal volume.

"I'll get 911," Stephen said.

Swallowing, I reached out and touched Roger's shoulder.

It would be the last time.

CHAPTER 2

I SAT ON ROGER'S COUCH UNTIL THE POLICE CAME, TRYING not to stare at what was left of him. Stephen played some video game on his phone. Every so often it let out a scream.

"Temple Run," he said. "This guy is running from demonic monkeys."

My head throbbed. "Can you at least turn it down?"

He tapped the screen. "Better?"

"Slightly."

There was a crash behind me. Twisting around, I saw one of Roger's ceramics on the floor, its stand toppled and its glazed white clay shattered. A thirtyish woman in a long, black leather coat stood over the carnage, swearing. Bending to pick up the pieces, she looked like Keanu Reeves in *The Matrix*, but with slightly more estrogen.

A fiftyish uniformed male officer came in, holding his belt as if it were incapable of keeping his pants up.

She stood. "Take care of this, would you?"

Frowning, he pulled an evidence bag from his pocket, knelt, and started cleaning up the mess.

The woman held a walleted badge in front of my nose. "Detective Jordan Spiner. Did you call this in?"

Stephen shut down his phone. "That was me." He spelled out his name.

"Either of you see what happened?"

I shook my head. "It was over before we got here. I'm Carolyn Neville. Spelled like it sounds."

She stuck the badge in her right pocket and pulled a pad from the left. "Who wants to go first?"

"*She* does," Stephen said. "Closer to the victim."

Spiner folded her arms. "How close?"

"Not as close as I'd hoped."

She pulled up a chair, turned it around, and straddled it. Who was she, that guy with the crewcut on *Law & Order: SVU?* I didn't like her already.

"He was a lawyer, right?"

"Yes."

"In charge of everything?"

"The Legal Department."

She wrote something down. "Tough gig. Lawyers and bosses have more enemies than saints and street people. Can you name me some of his?"

Stephen cackled. "How many pages on that pad?"

"Let me worry about that."

"There was this military guy with an artificial leg. Drove Carolyn nuts."

"Major Dijon," I said. "Buck. Wanted us to publish his poetry collection. We were going to do his exposé on cyberwarfare, but the government said it leaked classified material. Roger tried to defend him, but the head of the NSA was a very private person. When we deep-sixed the book, Buck blamed Roger."

She kept writing. I just wanted to go home, but Roger deserved better.

"Peggy Van Plugh was Roger's secretary," I continued. "Rumor had it she'd written him a note accusing him of leading her on. She said it was forged."

The uniformed officer got up, holding the evidence bag. "Where do you want this?"

"I'll take it," the detective said. "Insurance company might like it." She paused. "Anybody else?"

"First time we had dinner, Roger mentioned he had a personal trainer."

"How'd *that* come up?"

"Don't recall. Elaine something. Threatened to expose Roger for bribing a jury member. He denied it."

"Is that it?"

"Used to have a paralegal working for him. Mentioned her on our first date. Said she was fired for spending too much time on the Internet and not enough researching the statutes. Think he brought it up because she was a stalker. Thought I'd understand her because I'm a woman. But I don't."

The detective picked up the bag and glanced at the contents. "Did he give you any examples of her behavior?"

"No, but the second time we went out somebody keyed his car. Maybe she did it."

Spiner put down the bag. "Other coworkers?"

"Well, Gina Casebeer. Best lawyer in the department. Roger didn't give her enough credit, but she'd never kill anyone."

"Don't forget the old guy," Stephen said.

"Martin Curry?" I asked.

"Weird sense of humor, but seems harmless enough. Before passing the bar he was a Catskills comedian. Jokes so stale you could use them as frisbees. If they were bagels."

The detective made one more note. "I'm not writing down the bagel thing. That's just plain stupid."

He looked hurt. "It's not anti-Semitic. Even though he's Jewish."

"Since when is Curry a Jewish name?"

"You'd have to ask him."

She stuffed the pad in her pocket. "Is there anybody who *didn't* want to kill Trumbull? Our suspect list is already too long."

"*I* certainly didn't want him to die," I said.

Stephen shrugged. "Me neither."

She handed me her card. "You're free to go. We'll talk again."

Checking her watch, Spiner turned to the officer. "Find out where the coroner is. We haven't got all day."

I put the card in my purse. Stephen and I walked out the door, avoiding a few fragments of porcelain in our path. I tried not to think of the body behind me. Or the future I'd lost.

"We need to help Gina," I said. "With the Rosenthal thing. I owe her one. And Roger."

"How?"

"Don't know. But we'd better turn into multitaskers as soon as possible."

* * *

Next day we parked in a crowded lot on West 45th Street. The marquee of the Al Hirschfeld Theatre read KATHLEEN ROSENTHAL IN *MUCH ADO ABOUT SOMETHING*.

The matinee crowd was just leaving, hailing taxis and yelling at DON'T WALK signs that refused to change.

"I love Al Hirschfeld," Stephen said as we walked

toward the entrance. "World's greatest caricaturist. Except for Mort Drucker. Ever see his take on Richard Burton?"

"Probably."

"Always hid his daughter's name in his pictures. Nina. People counted them."

"Some folks aren't as busy as they ought to be."

"Hirschfeld lived to be a hundred. Kept drawing the whole time."

"Great. Let's see if we can find Kathleen."

Fighting the flow of theater patrons, we rounded the corner. I looked for the stage door. "Not even sure actors do this anymore. Some used to come out and sign autographs after shows."

Behind the brick building we found an old sign saying AUTHORIZED PERSONNEL ONLY. A knot of middle-aged fans gathered at the base of the steps, waving programs. We hung back, waiting. Finally a guy with big headphones around his neck came out and held up his hands. "Miss Rosenthal is sorry, but she's a little under the weather. She'd love to meet you sometime."

There was a groan, but it was polite. This wasn't a mob of rugby enthusiasts.

"We love you, Kathleen!" a stout, gray-haired lady shouted.

"I'll tell her," the guy said. The crowd dispersed with a collective sigh.

I ran up to the door and waved my arms.

"Like I said, Ma'am, she can't—"

"Kathleen knows us. Tell her it's Carolyn and Stephen from Pendleton House. It's about her book."

He looked doubtful. "If I'm not back in two minutes, assume it's a no." He disappeared inside and pulled the gray steel door tight.

"Have you seen the reviews for this show?" Stephen asked.

"Uh-uh. Must be decent. Pretty big turnout for a matinee."

"Better than *Spider-Man: Turn Off the Dark.*"

"Fewer injuries, too."

Our courier got back just before the deadline. "She can give you a few minutes." He waved us inside.

Down a hall lined with prop sofas and piles of wrinkled togas we followed. The place smelled like sweat and fresh paint.

The guy stopped and rapped on a dressing room door. There was actually a star on it, but no name.

"That you, Kevin?" said a voice from inside.

He pushed the door open. "They're here."

We walked past him.

She sat at a makeup table, wiping off foundation and brushing her auburn hair. Her toga had been replaced by jeans and a burgundy blouse, showing off a lithe figure that screamed *Gwyneth Paltrow.*

"Shouldn't take long," I said. "Don't want to disturb you."

She took a swig of bottled water. "Just a headache. Keep forgetting to hydrate. And the ibuprofen doesn't work like it used to, especially when I forget my soliloquy in Act Two."

"We've seen your manuscript. We know the legal problems. But something's happened. Have you met Roger Trumbull from the Legal Department?"

"Robert Redford."

"That's the one. Unfortunately, he was murdered last night."

"My God. Why?"

"That's what the police are asking. Awful lot of

suspects. You know two of them, I think. Your ex-husband and Martin Curry."

She rubbed her temples with her fingers. "If you've read the book, you know Joey was abusive. I've got no physical evidence; he managed not to leave scars. But I remember a show I was in with Martin. About seven years ago. *Little Miss Crumpet*. Do you know it?"

"Afraid not."

"Hardly anybody does. Closed after three performances. But Martin may have overheard us fighting in my dressing room."

"Any other witnesses?"

Shaking her head, she winced. "Think I need to lie down."

"Of course. Thanks for your time." I started to back out.

"Break a leg," Stephen said.

She took another drink. "Feels like I already did."

We showed ourselves out. Passing a golden arch, Stephen ran a finger across its face.

"Oh, crap," he said. "So that's where the wet-paint smell came from. Can't they put *signs* on this stuff?"

I took a tissue from my purse and handed it to him. "Everything you touch turns to gold, doesn't it?"

He scrubbed at his finger. "Next stop, Martin Curry. Right?"

"You know me so well. And I you."

"I guess there's no way to undo that."

"Not yet, but let's keep trying."

* * *

Martin's office looked more like a novelty shop than a lawyer's lair.

A black top hat and red-eyed rubber rabbit sat among the crumpled papers and worn-down pencils on his desk, which was stained with rings from his WORLD'S GREATEST UNCLE coffee mug. Next to a louvered closet hung autographed photos of Martin with Milton Berle and Imogene Coca, slightly askew. A rumpled clown suit, complete with shoes the size of scuba flippers, lay in a nearby chair.

There was a *bump* noise from under the desk, then an *ow*. Martin emerged, grimacing and smoothing back his thinning white hair. "Lost my contact," he said.

With a grunt he climbed into his chair and closed one eye. "Who needs 3D vision? At my age, I'm lucky to see anything."

"Those clown shoes are pretty amazing," I said.

He glanced in their direction. "Doing my nephew's birthday party next Saturday. Bargain-basement Ronald McDonald. Tough crowd, these kids today. Balloon horses don't impress them anymore. They want something called Solomon the Hedgehog."

"Sonic," Stephen corrected.

"Which reminds me of a Borscht-Belt joke I borrowed from the great Henny Youngman. 'I've got two wonderful children. And two out of five isn't too bad.'"

He held for laughs. It wasn't necessary.

"Martin, we're trying to figure out Roger's murder."

He shook his head. "Who isn't? Such a terrible thing. The man was a saint."

"We were just talking with Kathleen Rosenthal."

"A dear girl. How is she doing?"

"She had a headache. But she told us the two of you were in a show once."

"Ah, yes. *Little Miss Doughnut.*"

"*Little Miss Crumpet,*" Stephen said.

"Did you ever meet her husband, Joey?" I asked. "The one who wants us to kill her book?"

"Oh, did I ever. After one performance I heard the two fighting. And I'm not just talking argument. I was outside her dressing room. Suddenly the door flies open and he storms out. Said something I can't repeat in present company. Flew down the hall like the Von Trapps from the Nazis."

"Then what?"

"I went in. She was sitting on the floor, crying. Holding her arm. Had a bruise on it later, as I recall. The man was an animal."

"Would you testify to that in court?"

He opened both eyes wide. "I may be an old man, but I don't want to spend my declining years in a full-body cast."

I bit my lip. "Would you at least think about it?"

He picked up the rabbit and put it in the hat. Then he pulled it out.

"If it doesn't work out, could you make me vanish?"

"If it doesn't work out, we may *all* disappear."

CHAPTER 3

"Let's tell Gina," I said. "Where is she?"

Martin looked around and shrugged. "Hasn't come in today."

I took out my phone, dialed her at home, and put her on speaker. She answered, but just barely.

"Did I wake you up?"

"Almost."

"You sound terrible."

"Sleepy."

"But I've got good news. Martin may be willing to back up Kathleen's story."

"Uh-huh." There was a pause. "I mean, that's great."

"Are you contagious?"

"No."

"Then we'll come over to your place. Should we bring some chicken soup?"

"Afraid that wouldn't help."

She hung up.

"She sounds weird," Stephen said.

Gina had an apartment on the East Side. She buzzed

us in but didn't answer the door when we knocked. It was open, so I pushed it. I could hear it sliding as Roger's had, on the carpet. "Déja vu," I whispered.

She was sitting on the couch, staring at the wall. Her red glasses couldn't hide the circles under her eyes. She held a cup of tea in both hands, as if trying to warm them.

"The police think I'm probably the last person to see Roger alive."

"Opportunity," Stephen whispered.

"Shut up," I said.

She sipped the tea. "Guess you know I've always been overworked, underpaid, and uncredited."

"Pretty obvious."

"But I didn't tell the police."

"Motive," Stephen mumbled.

I ignored him.

"Gina, what happened that night?"

"I don't remember."

"How could you not?"

She put the cup down. "I passed out."

"As in drunk?" Stephen asked.

"No. I've got narcolepsy."

"Sleeping sickness," he said.

I shook my head. "That's something you get from tsetse flies. In Africa."

"Oh."

I turned to Gina. "Surely you remember *something*."

She cradled her face in her hands. "I was planning on working late. Roger discovered a mistake he'd made in the Rosenthal case." She looked up. "A file was open on my desk. I started to feel drowsy and put my head down. But I heard something."

"What?"

"Somebody coming in. Or out. No, in. To his office. Right before I lost consciousness. Whoever it was left and closed the door."

Rising stiffly to her feet, she stepped to the nearest closet. "I didn't show the police this."

She pulled the door open and took out a Whole Foods bag, then placed it on the couch. A fist-sized red stain was on the side, just above the green carrot design.

A box of Kleenex sat on the coffee table. She snatched one and wrapped it around whatever was in the bag.

Lip trembling, she lifted a knife—the kind my dad had used in Idaho to gut cutthroat trout.

"Found this in my purse," she said.

* * *

Judging from the silence, nobody knew what to say. I certainly didn't.

Gina held the knife out as if it were Excalibur. Blood was starting to soak through the tissue.

"Never seen it before."

I blinked several times, hoping to snap myself out of my reverie. I felt like she looked.

"Got any Ziplock bags?" I asked.

She placed the weapon on the coffee table and sank into the couch. "Second drawer down, left of the sink, in front of the waxed paper."

Dazed, I made my way to the kitchen and opened the drawer. I reached in and cut my palm on the serrated edge of the plastic wrap. After fishing out a bag, I returned to the living room and sealed in the knife.

Gina was staring straight ahead again. I sat next to her and stroked her arm. "Maybe somebody's trying to frame you," I whispered.

"But who would—"

There was a knock at the door. Stephen opened it.

Detective Spiner held up her badge. "Oh, it's you."

"You make it sound like a bad thing."

Another officer, an out-of-shape middle-aged guy with curly black hair, looked over her shoulder. His right hand rested on the gun in his holster.

Spiner pushed past Stephen. "Gina Marie Casebeer?"

She nodded, still watching the bag as if she could will it out of existence. "That's me."

Spiner held up a sheet of paper. "Got a search warrant."

"Guess you won't have to look far."

She picked up the bag and Spiner took it.

"Don't say anything, Gina," I counseled.

"I *know*. I'm a lawyer."

For a moment her eyes closed. She tottered forward.

I caught her. Her eyelids fluttered.

"Narcolepsy," I told Spiner.

"Not the same as sleeping sickness," Stephen said.

The detective handed the bag to the other cop. She looked at Gina. "Makes you pass out?"

"Yeah."

"Okay, let's do this right. You're under arrest for the murder of Roger Trumbull. You have the right to remain silent and refuse to answer questions. Anything you say may be used against you in a court of law. You have the right to consult an attorney before—"

"I know how it goes."

"Fine." She took out a pair of handcuffs.

"Oh, come on," I said. "Do you really need those?"

Spiner hesitated. "You might need to get a sweater. Go ahead."

Gina trudged to the closet, found a light green cardigan, and tugged it on.

She offered her wrists. Spiner snapped on the cuffs.

Suddenly Gina's eyes rolled up and her legs buckled. The uniformed cop jumped forward, but he was too late.

Her knees hit the carpet, followed by the side of her face.

* * *

Squatting beside the unconscious Gina, I felt for a pulse.

Spiner shook her head. "Relax. She's not dead. Just sleeping, right?"

"This is insane. Take the cuffs off. It's not like she's resisting arrest."

She shrugged. "Go ahead," she told her colleague in blue. "Last thing I need is another Internal Affairs charge of police brutality."

"*Another?*" I cried, getting up.

"All a misunderstanding."

Gina stirred, then groaned.

The cop slipped off her bonds. He looked sorry but said nothing.

Gina felt her cheek and sat up. "*Ow*. How long was I out?"

"Maybe a minute." I reached out, took her arm and helped her stand. She swayed like a newborn colt getting to its feet.

"We still have to take you in," Spiner said. "There's a probable murder weapon. And a motive. One of your coworkers confirmed that Trumbull treated you badly."

"Who?"

"Can't say."

I wanted to grab the knife myself and carve a few designs on Ms. Matrix, but it didn't seem very spiritual.

"I'll help pack your things," I told Gina.

I put my arm around her shoulder. We walked to her bedroom.

"Carolyn, what was it like?"

"They don't let you bring much. And the outfits are awful."

We picked out two sets of underwear, a jacket, some mouthwash, and several prescription bottles from her medicine cabinet. She put them in a bag from Old Navy.

"Can't believe I'm doing this," she said, her voice quivering.

"Jail isn't as bad as some people think," I said.

I knew it was even worse.

CHAPTER 4

THE METROPOLITAN CORRECTIONAL CENTER IN Manhattan looked pretty much like every other prison I'd ever seen—except for Alcatraz, which had a lot more character. A fortress of gray concrete, it rose from the street like a bureaucrat's attempt at a castle, minus the turrets and moats.

Stephen and I drove there the following morning. He poked his phone. "Too bad Gina couldn't go to the Motchan Detention Center on Riker's Island. It used to take women, but not anymore."

I searched for a parking space. "What's so great about it?"

"It's not the Metropolitan."

"What's that supposed to mean?"

"Some people call the Metropolitan 'the Guantanamo of New York'. Pretty severe security measures."

My hunt wasn't going well, which made me crankier. "Figures. Gina's obviously a hardened criminal."

It took at least ten minutes and a lot of horn-honking to find a place to squeeze into. When we got out, I squinted up at the building. "Reminds me of the King County Jail in Seattle, only bigger." I sniffed the air. "And in Seattle, the food trucks didn't smell like hot dogs and mustard. All fried clams and crepes."

We surrendered our contraband, like smartphones and pepper spray, at the front desk. The elevator took us to the fourth floor, where we sat in front of a plexiglass shield and waited.

A female guard with a jawbone like a Tyrannosaurus, and beady eyes to match, led Gina in by the shoulder and pointed at the inmate's chair. Gina looked like she hadn't shut her eyes in a week, but at least there were no handcuffs. The guard stepped back three paces.

I picked up our phone. Gina grasped hers.

I made a halfhearted attempt at smiling. "Brings back fond memories."

It was all she could do to keep her head up. "Something like that. Kind of reverses the situation in Seattle, doesn't it?"

"You got *me* out. Maybe this time I can return the favor."

"Appreciate that, but I need a good lawyer. Ever heard of Alexander Washington? Roger thought he was another Clarence Darrow. Not sure I can afford him."

"We'll figure that out later. In any case, I owe you one."

Stephen leaned back in his chair. "When I get my phone back, I'll look him up."

I took a pad from my purse. "We need more suspects. Up to a few questions?"

She nodded.

"How did Roger treat his other employees?"

"Liza Boxer used to be our paralegal. Roger fired her

for spending all her time on the Internet. Can't say she didn't deserve it."

I scribbled notes. "We know about Martin Curry and Peggy Van Plugh."

"Elaine Jeong was Roger's personal trainer. Just met her once. She was yelling at him. Saying he'd bribed a jury member. Didn't say when. She was going to expose him. Roger denied it. Never could understand why he needed a trainer in the first place. They parted ways after that."

"When did they have that conversation?"

She looked up at the ceiling, thinking. "Maybe six months ago."

I scribbled again.

The guard checked her watch. "Time's almost up."

Sighing, I stowed the pad in my purse. "Gina, I wish I could—"

"That's okay." Her eyelids drooped.

"We'll be back."

Stephen cleared his throat. "In the meantime, let me lighten things up by quoting one of Martin Curry's jokes."

She yawned. "Sure I've heard all of them."

"Oh. Well, I've got a few others. Five guys come into a bar. A minister, a priest, a rabbi, a Muslim imam, and a Buddhist monk. They're arguing about how the universe came to be. The minister says it was six-day Creation. The priest says it was the Big Bang. The rabbi says theistic evolution. The Muslim says it was a miracle. The Buddhist says the question is unanswerable. They decide to ask the bartender. He puts down a glass and—"

I looked at Gina. Her head listed toward her left shoulder. She was snoring.

The guard stepped forward, roused her, and started

to lead her away. She managed to wave sadly with her free hand. I did the same.

Stephen slumped in his chair. "Can I tell you the rest?"

I shook my head. "Have to stay alert. I'm driving, remember?"

* * *

They gave us back our contraband on the way out. We were almost to the car when Stephen said, "Eureka!"

"You found Gina's lawyer? Alexander Hamilton?"

"*Washington.* His office is about half an hour from here. Want to go?"

"We can sign him up later. First we need something to tell him."

"We have plenty already."

"Look up Buck Dijon."

"Your favorite poet. Don't you have him on speed dial?"

"What I need is a restraining order."

He wiped his finger all over the screen of the phone, searching. "Got his address. In Brooklyn."

I pulled into traffic. "Have you ever met the Major?"

"Thanks to you, no. His reputation precedes him."

"Looks more like Dwayne Johnson than Walt Whitman. Tough guy. One leg's artificial. Lost the real one in Iraq."

"How?"

"Doesn't talk about it. Got a touch of PTSD, if you ask me. Maybe the poems are his way of letting off steam."

Stephen looked out the window. "Take the next right

and go about twenty-five blocks. He's in Fort Greene. Sounds pretty military."

"Actually, it's pretty artsy. Guess he wants to play both sides of the street."

When we got there, it was clear the place was gentrified. Fern bars and delis lined Myrtle Avenue. Half the people dressed like average New Yorkers, but the rest favored tie-dyed shirts and camouflage.

I looked for a place to park, but saw only bicycles.

"One of those pedestrian malls," Stephen said. "Cars are verboten."

After passing three buses, I crossed the line into fossil fuel country. A space opened up on the right just as we approached.

"Take it!" Stephen said. "We'll have to walk, but it could be our last chance."

I pulled up to the curb and got out some change.

"The brick place past the Chipotle. That's where he lives."

I fed the meter. "We'll have to talk fast. Only have a few quarters."

We made our way down the sidewalk. Kids on Big Wheel tricycles did circles around us, the plastic tires scraping the cement. A woman with a bulldog on a leash scowled at them.

Stephen passed me and halted at the intercom on the Major's building. "This is it."

I bent to read a tiny bronze plaque next to the intercom. DIJON, it said. I pressed the button.

There was a popping sound. "Identify yourself," said that officious voice I'd come to know and avoid.

"Carolyn Neville. From—"

The speaker buzzed. "Proceed."

"Creepy," Stephen whispered. "Hope he doesn't mind an unauthorized visitor."

"Don't make any sudden moves. Wouldn't be surprised if he's got an AK-47."

"A poet with an assault weapon?"

"Carl Sandburg had a sharp stick. Read it somewhere."

We took the elevator to the third floor. Apartment 7B sported a golden knocker with the Eagle, Globe, and Anchor of the United States Marines. Taking hold of the anchor, I tapped it against the wood.

I could hear a rhythmic stride advance in my direction. Locks and latches clicked. "Enter," barked the Major, and the door swung open.

I found myself looking at a chest as broad as I was tall. He was clothed in a white linen suit over a gray shirt with no collar. Brown eyes narrowing, he stepped aside.

"I have a poem for you."

"Can't wait."

He nodded at Stephen. "Friend of yours?"

"Not exactly."

We slipped past him. Stephen kept looking at the Major's legs, which resembled the columns of the Lincoln Memorial.

"Which one's the fake?" Stephen whispered.

"Don't ask. He can kick your butt with either one."

"Please sit down," the Major said. It was more a command than an invitation.

We complied. I crossed my legs and waited.

"Ready?" he asked.

"As I'll ever be."

Putting his hands behind his back, he assumed the *ten-hut* position and cleared his throat.

Flaming voyage, death's head boat,
Rotting hounds and feral cats,
Rockets fired on remote,
Illicit caves of vampire bats;
You thought you came to slay the beast,
To be the main course at the feast,
But nightmares come to those who wait,
Who fear to question Adam's fate,
Who all remember and still jest
At warriors fallen in their quest.
Let those who sacrificed the most
To satisfy the hellish host
Retreat in safe paternity
A quantum leap, eternity.

I stared, fumbling for a comment that wasn't uncomplimentary or true. "That's one of the most—"

He held up his palm. "Wait. There's more."

"I can only absorb so much greatness at one time."

Stephen just sat there, trying to keep a straight face.

The Major nodded, then sat. "So what do you think?"

"That's a new one?" I asked.

"Wrote it two days ago."

"It's certainly consistent with your existing body of work. Uplifting. Inspiring."

"Not too suggestive?"

Stephen raised an eyebrow.

"Didn't even occur to me," I said.

"Good. I think this puts my collection over the top. I know we've discussed this before, but the time has come to publish. The market for cryptic but insightful military poetry will soon mushroom like an unintended nuclear detonation."

I turned to Stephen. "What do you think?"

He turned pale, perhaps recalling my comment about firearms. "Uh . . . Where were you when Roger Trumbull was killed?"

The Major's eyes flashed. "*What?*"

"You know. An alibi. Do you have one?"

"No, but I have a Kimber 1911 RAPIDE Custom pistol."

Stephen looked at me. "Must not be him. Murder weapon was a knife."

"My colleague's just doing his job. Or, rather, the police's. We know you have a motive."

He got up, crossed the room, and opened a red cedar box on an antique buffet.

"Gun!" Stephen whispered.

Buck reached into the box, took out a USB drive, and held it up. "This is the backup of *Gallant Hearts, Grim Horizons*."

"The book Roger allowed to be cancelled," I said.

"None of it was classified. Not a *word*."

He flung the drive against the wall.

"Poetry slam," Stephen said. "First time I've—"

The Major swore and took three steps toward him. "Ever seen a compound fracture?"

"Does Silly Putty count? Shatters at thirty-two degrees Fahrenheit."

He picked up the drive and tossed it back in the box. "What about the book?"

"Doesn't meet our current needs. We wish you the best in placing it elsewhere."

"I can think of a place I'd like to put it, if it were printed and bound."

"Thank God it's not."

I grabbed Stephen's wrist. "Looks like our work here is done."

* * *

We drove back to Manhattan. Stephen kept checking the rearview mirror.

"Must not be following. Can't see any Humvees."

"A little excitable, isn't he?"

"Knows how to find us, at least at the office."

I tapped the steering wheel. "I'll look into that restraining order. Get your own. I don't think they let you split the bill."

"Now what?"

I reached into my purse, keeping my eyes on the road. "I call Spiner."

She picked up. Didn't sound happy to hear from me, though.

"Just talked to Major Dijon."

"And?"

"He's as fond of me as ever. Have you found any physical evidence in Roger's office?"

"Can't comment on that. Look, Jessica Fletcher, I'm in the middle of a stakeout."

"Then this is the perfect time to talk."

She muttered something Jessica would never tolerate, but I did.

"What about fingerprints?" I asked.

"We've found plenty. Everybody who worked for him seems to have touched his desk. Computer keyboard, chair arms, light switches. Big help."

"Anything else?"

"Hold on. Looks like our person of interest just got a lot more interesting."

There was a fumbling noise. What sounded like a car door opened, then slammed.

"Crap," she said. "False alarm. You were saying?"

"Fingerprints."

She laughed. "The old guy, Martin Curry, left so many prints it had to be on purpose."

"What do you make of that?"

"Nothing."

I sighed. "Keep us posted, okay?"

"No law says I have to."

Stephen motioned for me to give him the phone. "We were just talking. Maybe you can clear something up. Do you handle restraining orders?"

"Are you kidding? I'm a detective, not a paper pusher."

"Just tell me the rules."

She made an exasperated noise. "Where's the offender live?"

"Brooklyn."

"Get an Order of Protection in Kings County. Go to court to file the petition. Fill out a bunch of forms."

Turning to me, he snapped his fingers. "Need something to write with."

I handed him my pad and pen.

"Okay. Order of Protection. Kings County. File petition. Bunch of forms."

"A judge will review your petition. Then there's a hearing."

"Is that it?"

"That's just the *beginning*. And this is the end."

She hung up.

CHAPTER 5

TRAFFIC WAS LIGHT ON THE WAY BACK TO THE OFFICE. IT was starting to rain. When we passed a Wendy's, Stephen scrabbled at the passenger window with his fingers like a drowning man.

"Haven't eaten for three hours."

"Can't hear your stomach growling over the windshield wipers."

"Have mercy. Just a Junior Double Cheeseburger."

"Suppose you'll insist on a Frosty, too."

"A small one. Chocolate. On me."

"If you're careful, it won't be. I've got a napkin in the glove compartment."

"Can we go back?"

"Next exit, I promise. Probably won't be Wendy's, though."

Sighing, he pressed his nose to the window like a famished beagle.

"Don't lick the glass," I said.

The rain beat down harder. I cranked up the wipers. The rhythm didn't seem to soothe him.

"There," he said as we approached a green EXIT 264 sign. "McDonald's and Red Robin. You choose."

I eased off the highway. Golden arches glowed in the distance. Couldn't see any signs with scarlet avians, so I went for the sure thing.

Stephen ordered a Big Mac, large fries, and strawberry shake. I stuck with a Garden Salad and iced coffee.

"How can you eat that stuff?" I asked after we sat down.

"Pickles are a vegetable. Strawberries are fruit." He sucked so hard on his straw that his cheeks caved in and his eyes bugged out.

"We haven't made our usual list of suspects," I said. "Not officially."

He dipped a fry in a puddle of ketchup. "Don't let me stop you."

I went back to the counter and returned with a McDonald's Coloring Page and a little box of crayons. Mayor McCheese and the Hamburglar begged to be filled in, but I turned the sheet over and went to work.

- *GINA CASEBEER*
- *MAJOR BUCK DIJON*
- *PEGGY VAN PLUGH*
- *MARTIN CURRY*
- *ELAINE JEONG*
- *LIZA BOXER*

"Nice penmanship," he said, unwrapping his Big Mac. "Considering the medium."

I popped the lid off my salad. "Is that it?"

His mouth was full, so he just nodded.

"This must be the longest list we've ever had," I said.

He swallowed. "We've only talked with a few of them."

Returning to the counter, I grabbed two straws and placed them in the middle of our table. "Now, each of these is a suspect. This one's Elaine Jeong. Here's Liza Boxer."

I took a sip of coffee. "Now close your eyes and pick one."

His hand hovered over the straws. I took the opportunity to steal a French fry.

"This one," he said, and opened his eyes.

"It's Liza."

"*What's* Liza?"

"The next one we talk to."

"Oh. Can I finish my food?"

"If you don't stroke out first from all that cholesterol."

He looked down at his fries. "Hey, one of these is missing."

"You *counted* them?"

"Doesn't everybody?"

"No. You're paranoid."

"And you've got ketchup on your fingers."

"Mystery solved. One down, one to go."

* * *

Liza lived in a small apartment with a little yippie dog. We could hear it through the door.

"I know," I told Stephen. "You *hate* dogs. At least this one sounds too small to reach your groin and sniff it."

"If it jumps on my lap, I won't be responsible for my actions."

I knocked three times. The yipping got yippier.

"On my way," Liza sang. A chain slid.

She was in her mid-twenties. Looked like one of the Campbell Soup twins, baby-faced, rosy, with cheeks like Mrs. Santa Claus and an apron like Julia Child used to wear. The canine, a white chihuahua, nosed around the doorframe and growled.

"Roger, get down," Liza admonished.

"You named a *dog* after him?" Stephen asked.

"Liza," I said. "I'm Carolyn Neville. From Pendleton House. This is Stephen."

She picked Roger up and opened the door wider. "Oh, I remember. I helped you with a copyright question once. Before I got fired."

Inside, the salmon pink walls were covered with photos of her pet dressed in costumes. Police dog. Judge. Banana.

"I take pictures of him with the outfits on. I sew them myself."

"That's a great Thomas Jefferson," Stephen said. "How'd you get him to hold still for the wig?"

"Played the soundtrack from *1776*. The "Mama, Look Sharp" song was like rubbing him on the tummy."

She kissed her pet on top of his head. "Got a YouTube channel where I post the images. Hasn't made any money yet. Need more subscribers. And I'm trying to sell more costumes on Etsy."

"Mind if we sit?" I asked.

"Go right ahead. I was just in the middle of felting when I heard the door."

"Felting?"

"You take fibers like wool and compress them, then shape them into puppets or dolls. Even dogs. I'm working on a Roger. But don't tell him. It's a surprise."

Stephen looked sideways at me. He didn't make the

rotate-your-finger-next-to-your temple "crazy" gesture, but I knew what he was thinking.

"Would you like some bilk?" she asked.

"Bilk?"

"Beer and milk. Didn't invent it, but I've added certain . . . refinements."

Clapping his hand over his mouth, he puffed out his cheeks as if ready to barf.

"Maybe some other time," I said.

Liza sat. So did we. The dog settled into her lap, twitching.

"Now, about this firing—"

"He said I spent too much time on the Internet. Not enough researching laws. Probably thought I was trying to start my business on company time, but I wasn't."

The dog started whimpering, vibrating.

"I don't hold it against him. If he hadn't let me go, I might not have gotten the courage to go out on my own."

"Are you always this forgiving?"

Stroking the dog, she smiled. "Yes, I think so. I've tried to—"

Suddenly she flinched and stopped. I hadn't noticed the blue fabric brace on her wrist. "Carpal tunnel syndrome. From all the kneading and felting, but especially the knitting. Very repetitive."

"So there *are* some things you can't do," I said.

"Like stabbing," Stephen suggested.

She giggled. "You're funny."

The dog jumped down and trotted toward the kitchen.

Liza followed, then returned with a box of cookies shaped like cats and birds. "I can still do cookies. You don't knead them. They get too crispy and thin."

She handed her creations to Stephen. "Care for a sample?"

"Wow, thanks." He looked sheepish. "Sorry about the stabbing thing."

"They go perfectly with bilk."

He gulped. "I'll take a pint."

She found a mason jar and filled it.

We spent the next ten minutes eating small animals. Stephen didn't touch his drink.

I rose to leave. "Good luck with your felting."

"Great cookies," Stephen said.

Out in the hall I failed to stifle a laugh. "New girlfriend, eh?"

"She's not my type."

"What type is that?"

"Normal."

* * *

I spent the next morning at my desk, putting out the usual fires. An agent named Donald had spent the last six months pitching me a sequel to *For Whom the Bell Tolls*. He called me again. "Tentative title: *The Bellman Rings Twice*. See? Literary allusion."

"The answer's still no."

I started to hang up, but he beat me to it. In the spirit of forgiveness, I fired up Microsoft Outlook and deleted him from my Contacts list.

My phone rang. It was Hunter's admin. "You-know-who wants to see you and Stephen at three."

"What's it about?"

"Report on the Rosenthal book."

For once I didn't mind. We'd actually made progress. I hoped the shock wouldn't be too much.

At 2:57 I swung by Stephen's cubicle. He was eating the last cat cookie from Liza, a bright orange tabby. "Time to dazzle the boss with our prowess," I said. "Come on."

Hunter wasn't practicing golf swings this time. He was sitting at his desk, playing with one of those executive timewasters, a pendulum with magnetic stainless steel balls. He pulled back the nearest one and let it go. With a *click* it transferred the energy to the one that was furthest and sent the latter flying.

"You seem troubled," I said. *Suicidal* might have been a better word.

He looked up. "I'm still stunned over Roger."

"We all are. But I've got good news."

He leaned back in his chair. "Don't toy with me."

"No toying. We met with Martin Curry. He's willing to back up Kathleen's story."

"Wow. He never struck me as particularly brave."

"He's not. But he's old. Maybe figures he's got nothing to lose."

He sighed. "Didn't know Roger all that well. But we had something in common."

"Generosity and eloquence?" Stephen asked.

"That goes without saying. But I was thinking of his commitment to fitness. We shared a personal trainer."

"Elaine Jeong," I said.

He nodded. "She has a certain . . . *joie de vivre*."

"Joy of living?"

"No, that's not it." He scratched his chin. "Musk, I think."

Stephen snickered.

"*Musk?*" I asked. "Like she needs deodorant?"

"It's more of a scent. Utterly female. Powerful. Attractive. What do they call it?"

"Pheromones," I said.

"Heckuva fencer, too. Taught me how to flunge."

Stephen took out his phone. "I think you mean *lunge*."

"Look it up."

Seconds later, Stephen shrugged. "We're both right. They're attacking moves. But you've gotta admit lunging *sounds* better."

Hunter closed his eyes. "And when it comes to her body—"

"Hold it right there," I said. "Human Resources alert. For your own good, leave it to our imagination."

He grunted, then went back to clicking and clacking the pendulum. "Roger's memorial service is Friday. I expect you'll be there, of course."

"We will."

"I've been asked to make a few remarks."

"Really?"

"Is that so surprising?"

"I didn't know you two were that close."

"We weren't. Maybe they just wanted somebody . . . what's the word . . ."

"Articulate?"

"Right. Also, all upper managers have to say something."

There was silence, except for the clicking and clacking.

"You can go now," he said. "Got a ton of stuff to do."

"So I see."

Ignoring us, he leaned closer to the pendulum.

We headed for the door. Stephen turned back, bowed slightly, and said something that sounded like he was clearing phlegm from his throat.

"What was *that?*" I asked.

"Klingon salute," he said.

CHAPTER 6

"HUNTER'S JUST *WEIRD*," STEPHEN SAID AS WE HEADED toward our cars.

"Just noticed?" I asked, fishing keys from my purse.

"Oh, crap," Stephen said. "Some kind of accident."

I glanced up. Two squad cars, lights flashing. Four cops directing traffic. Two drivers talking on cellphones. A garbage truck with a Yellow taxi scrunched under it, looking ready to be hauled away.

We didn't need a KFRC radio traffic report to tell us we needed a different route.

"Cut through the alley," I said.

Wending our way through the honks and expletives, we ducked between filthy brick walls and tried to get oriented.

"We're two blocks west," Stephen said.

"Three blocks east."

He took out his phone.

"It doesn't know where we parked," I said. "Let's just follow our instincts. We'll start with mine."

We picked our way past a dumpster and an uncapped

50-gallon drum a Greek restaurant was using to collect grease. It smelled like orange peels and rancid saganaki cheese.

I coughed. "Now, if you look past that wino and to the right—"

Suddenly I heard footsteps behind me.

"Hold it," said a voice. Whirling, I faced a figure in black sweatsuit and matching bandana mask. Sounded like a woman, but I couldn't be sure. The slender, flat-chested physique provided no gender reveal.

"You know," he or she said, "you really ought to let the cops and lawyers handle the legal stuff."

I looked down at my hand. Still holding my keys. Weren't you supposed to use them as weapons at times like these? The pepper spray was unreachable, but—

"Is this a mugging, or what?" Stephen asked, sounding impatient.

"A warning," said our assailant.

"Where's your gun?"

"At home in a safe. I've got this." The androgynous ninja drew some kind of knife from its belt.

"Cool dagger."

"Not what it's called, but no matter. You getting my message?"

My keys being no match for the cutlery, I nodded. "You want us to stick to our editing and quit trying to find Roger's killer. A cliché, but fairly effective."

Stephen frowned. "Here's what I don't get. How'd you know we'd be in this alley?"

"Been following you. I know where you work, where you drive, and when. If you think I'll stop, forget it. Are we clear?"

"You're quite the communicator," I said.

"Go to your cars. I'll give you a thirty-second head start."

"*Then* what?"

The Phantom held up the knife and waggled it. "What do *you* think?"

I turned to Stephen. "We were just leaving, right?"

"Yeah."

"Youth before beauty."

"Does that mean—"

"Just *go*."

He started sprinting. I stole one more look at the Phantom, but he, she, or it was gone.

I caught up with Stephen as we neared the car. We were both panting.

"Remember what Hunter said about the personal trainer?" he asked.

"Can't be her. Too much of a coincidence. But eventually we'll have to talk with her."

"Maybe we just did."

* * *

The gridlock trapping our vehicles was breaking up. Siren wailing, the last squad car battled to get through traffic. The trash truck was gone. The taxi, too smashed for its wheels to spin, was on a flatbed. I could see an ambulance rounding a corner, probably taking the driver to Lenox Hill Hospital.

"Boy, that was no contest," Stephen said.

Sending up a quick prayer for the cabbie, I leaned against my car and dialed Spiner. While it rang, I crooked my finger and beckoned Stephen.

"Spiner," said the voice at the other end. I put her on speaker.

"Need to report a mugging," I said.

"Whose?"

"Ours. Well, more of a warning. We've still got our wallets."

"I don't usually handle this kind of report."

"But it could tie into Roger Trumbull's murder."

She sighed. "Give me a description."

"He or she was wearing a black sweatsuit and bandana-type mask. About five-eight, skinny. Sounded female, but couldn't be sure."

"Any accent?"

"Don't think so. Is *snotty* an accent?"

"More of an attitude. What did this mystery person say?"

"To give up on solving Roger's murder. Hazardous to our health."

"He or she's been watching too many old movies. Was a gun involved?"

"No, just a knife."

Stephen leaned toward the phone. "I'd call it a dagger. Kind of a ninja deal."

"Not much of a description. And this happened in broad daylight?"

"No witnesses. We were in an alley."

There was a rustling noise. Spiner mumbled to someone at the other end. Something like "get off your butt and call the judge's office".

"Do you know about Elaine Jeong?" Stephen asked.

"Uh . . . personal trainer?"

"Yeah. She was Roger's."

"She's done some martial arts classes for the department. Wouldn't want to meet her in the ring, much less an alley."

I took the phone back. "She accused Roger of bribing a jury member."

"That's news to me. What was the case?"

"Don't know yet."

Stephen leaned in again. "She could have been our mugger. Or warner. Whatever."

"Could you pick this individual out of a lineup?"

"Well, no."

"Any smell of cologne or perfume?"

"My olfactory lobe wasn't functioning."

I shook my head.

"Seems a little too obvious for the killer to dress up in a costume and threaten you directly," Spiner said. "Did the person do any karate chops or acrobatics?"

"No."

"Maybe somebody's trying to frame Jeong."

"Huh," Stephen mumbled. "Hadn't thought of that."

"I tell you what. After I do everything else on my list, which is about three feet long, I'll look into it. The jury-tampering case."

"Will you file a report?" I asked. "Isn't threatening with a deadly weapon a felony?"

She swore under her breath, but not so far under that I couldn't make it out. "I'll do that right after I shave my head and start selling flowers at LaGuardia."

"They still let you do that?"

"Nope."

* * *

"Why would anybody frame the trainer?" Stephen asked when we sat down to dinner at the tiniest hot dog place on Second Avenue, Schaller's Stube Sausage Bar. The menu said it was a former meat fridge. Stephen got two dogs and a beer. Not feeling Teutonic, I ordered the fried chicken and cream soda. Diet.

"Why not?" I asked. "She's the most muscular type on the list. Except for the Major."

Our food was ready before I could unwrap my plastic utensils and napkin. That's how it goes when you have only 10 tables and the lunch crowd is gone.

"Who haven't we talked with yet?" I asked, sticking a straw in my bottle. "Suspects, I mean."

"Roger's secretary."

"Peggy."

He bit into his first tube steak. He seemed to have some kind of seizure, eyes rolling into the back of his head. I looked away. The moment was too intimate to share.

"Gina told me about both of them," I said.

He managed to compose himself and picked up his pilsner. "Hard to believe Roger would lead Peggy on. She's sort of . . . *bovine.*"

"Are you saying she looks like a *cow?*"

"Not literally. Just a little like Melissa McCarthy."

"Pardon my feminism, but that's awfully sexist."

He burped. "My bad."

"Still, I have to agree Peggy sounds delusional."

"The *Fatal Attraction* type. She may not want to talk."

I sucked up the last of my drink. "Aren't you the guy who got us into that pharmaceutical company in the middle of the night? The one in Seattle, where Gina bailed you out?"

"No, that was you. Actually, it was the researcher who killed seagulls with her purse."

"Probably not available," he said.

"Then we'll have to do it ourselves. First thing tomorrow."

CHAPTER 7

On Friday, mid-morning, I drove us to Roger's memorial service. The church was a big one, its flagstone flanks veined with ivy. Very Episcopal. Very Roger.

Inside we were met by an unexpectedly happy-faced usher, young and female and handing out programs. Roger's face was on the cover, square-jawed and smiling, unaware that his time was just about up.

Stephen opened his bulletin and squinted at the order of service as if it were Sanskrit. "When I go, just turn me to ashes and give all the adults a Corona. Not that any kids would be there. Don't think I know any."

The place being packed, I took his elbow and led him toward a pew in the rear. "Want me to make any remarks at your funeral?"

"Thanks, but no. I'd like 'em to be positive."

I scanned the crowd for familiar faces, which is tough when everybody's facing frontward. Fortunately, there was nothing to see on the overhead screen, and most of the mourners were gazing around like tourists in the Sistine Chapel or whispering head-to-head.

The organist began to play something medieval. I spotted Martin Curry near the front, staring at a stained-glass window depicting Moses with the tablets. It was the most Jewish image in the place, except for the one with Jacob getting knocked off the ladder by an angel who looked like Hulk Hogan.

Peggy Von Plugh sat several rows in front of us, her nose in a hymnal. To the right, halfway back, was Liza Boxer. Her outfit was pink, with an Easterish hat whose brim was wide as a bicycle wheel. Not far away sat Spiner, who'd traded her long leather coat for a short one, equally black. I didn't see Dijon or Jeong.

When the dirge's last notes faded, a short man in a clerical collar took the pulpit, said his Dearly Beloveds, and asked for a moment of silence. My eyes fell on the casket before him, closed and ringed by enough floral arrangements to keep FTD in business for a month.

"And now," said the priest, "I would like to introduce our first speaker." He consulted a sheet of paper on the podium. "From the company where Roger worked, Pendleton House, his dear friend and co-worker, Mr. Hunter Thicke."

"Boy, is *he* misinformed," Stephen whispered.

His own notes in hand, Hunter mounted the platform. Head lowered, he managed to pass for solemn instead of just brain-damaged.

He cleared his throat. "Thank you, Padre, for that brief introduction. To give you some context, I should add that Roger and I were like brothers, or comrades-with-arms, or perhaps even clones. We shared a love for fine dining, for fitness and having books on our shelves. The *great* books, such as Shakespeare and Shelley Duvall and Louis L'Amour."

Pausing, he turned the sheet over. "When Roger's

wife passed away, I gave him some advice I would like to share with you. 'Seize the date,' I said. 'Save the tiger. Let no weekend be lost; when it comes to grief, let it go.' I had read this in *Bartlett's Familiar Quotations,* which I have mostly memorized despite the fact that our company didn't publish it. We do, however have the movie rights until 2037."

I looked over at Cornell Riggs, who was shaking his head and seemed to be stifling a laugh. The priest seemed confused and more than a little worried.

"So in closing," Hunter said, folding up his notes, "please remember the words of King George Hamilton the Fourth:

'I'll be back
Soon you'll see
You'll remember you belong to me
I'll be back
Time will tell
If you don't, then you can go to—'"

About seventy percent of the audience gasped, the rest having been lulled to sleep.

Panicky, the priest nodded vigorously at the organist, who attacked the keys like the Phantom of the Opera and started playing Hunter off the platform.

The latter gave a little bow, stuck the paper in his pocket, and returned to his seat.

"Roger must be turning over in his grave," Stephen whispered.

"Spinning," I mumbled.

A bit off balance, the cleric zigzagged to the podium and introduced the next speaker, some woman in Marketing.

I sank back against the pew.

"We should corner Peggy at the reception," I whispered.

Somewhere near the front, a woman swooned.

* * *

We found Peggy lingering over the refreshments, looking forlorn. She was staring at a window-sized, gold-framed photo of Roger on an easel. A single potato chip was in her hand.

I walked over and picked one up myself. "Peggy, isn't it?"

Her head slowly rotated in my direction. She popped the morsel in her mouth.

"I'm Carolyn Neville. The young man salivating over the little spinach tarts and summer sausage slices is Stephen Ames."

She nodded. "Seen you around the office. Talked over the phone, of course."

Stephen picked up a large paper plate and chose his targets carefully, carefully arranging them in concentric circles. The woman guarding the punchbowl, a skinny redhead wielding a clear plastic ladle as if it were Thor's hammer, gave him a dirty look.

I crunched my chip and took another, then nodded at the portrait. "Roger was a wonderful man, wasn't he? You were probably as close to him as anyone at work."

She snorted. "I hardly think so. Never went out with him, unlike certain editors who will remain nameless."

"But you wanted to, didn't you?"

"What makes you say that?"

Stephen stood behind her, his jaw working. He

pointed at the cocktail wieners on his plate and made the *OK* sign.

"I understand Gina Casebeer found a note to that effect. You felt he was toying with you. I could understand how that must make you—"

"It was forgery. I've never been interested in Roger. And what was Gina doing, snooping around like that? Frankly, I'm glad she's finally where she belongs."

I turned to the Bodyguard of Beverages. "One for me, please."

She looked me over as if trying to decide whether I was of age. Or so I hallucinated. Finally she filled one of those nubby glass teacups with what looked like the grape Kool-Aid Reverend Jim Jones urged his followers to drink in Guyana.

Stephen finished what he was chewing, then swallowed. "Peggy, why'd you come to the memorial service? I mean, it's not like you had any respects to pay him, last or otherwise."

"Loyalty."

I sipped my drink. Sickly sweet, but apparently not laced with cyanide. "Then I guess you'll be staying around to work for Roger's successor, whoever that turns out to be."

She took a cracker smeared with cream cheese. "I'm holding things together for the time being. Not that anybody's noticed." She slipped it between her lips and nibbled.

When the hors d'oeuvre was gone, she stepped over to the Potentate of Punch, nodded at the bowl, and snapped her fingers. The redhead looked shocked.

"No punch for *you*," she said.

Stephen leaned toward me. "See, it's like *Seinfeld*. There's a guy called the Soup Nazi, and—"

"I'm not a cultural illiterate."

Peggy's eyes narrowed. "Excuse me. I need to grieve in private."

"Not as crazy as I thought," Stephen said. "Maybe crazier."

He tossed his plate into a nearby can and started over.

CHAPTER 8

On our way out we bumped into Detective Spiner. Not literally. It was more like chasing, since she took one look at us and started fast-walking toward her car.

"Nice service, don't you think?" I called.

"Funerals aren't my thing. And your publishing friend was a jerk."

"We thought so, too." I paused. "Not all the suspects were here. What does that tell you?"

"Very little, since they all had a reason to kill him. Major Whathisname didn't show. Oh, and by the way—the trainer, Jeong, seems to have an alibi for the time of the murder, but not for the mugging."

"Knew it was her," Stephen said.

"You don't know any such thing," Spiner said. "Whoever the Phantom was, take his or her advice and leave this to the NYPD." She climbed into her car and took off.

"Hey!" cried a voice behind us. No need to turn around to know who it was, but I did anyway.

Liza Boxer carried a bag from Hobby Lobby. Her face was pinker than usual, rather moist. "How about those refreshments? Didn't you love those little cucumber-butter tea sandwiches?"

"Didn't have any," Stephen said, making a face.

She opened the bag. "I knitted this for you."

He took a step back and put up his palm, like Professor Van Helsing raising a crucifix in Dracula's face. "Oh, gee, a cap. Reminds me of my nephew. Two months old. Only his isn't lime green. It's blue. And smaller."

Beaming, Liza placed the abomination in his hand. "Try it on."

After searching the lot to make sure no one was watching, he pulled it over his ears and tried to smile. "Perfect," he said. "But I have a skin condition. Makes me allergic to wool."

"This is polyester."

"Right. They both make me break out in a rash."

She sighed. "Well, if you don't like it—"

"Love it. My English terrier will appreciate it even more. Mister Perry gets cold at night. I don't let him sleep on the bed."

I checked the urge to reveal that he'd rather own a pet cockroach than a dog.

Liza patted him on the arm and went back to the reception. For more finger sandwiches, I supposed.

We were almost to my car when I realized Martin Curry was leaning against the driver's side. He looked terrible, sweaty and gray. His right hand clutched his chest.

I gasped. "What's wrong? You look like you're having a heart attack."

"Ran out of pills. Timing is everything."

I took out my phone and dialed 911.

Martin took a deep breath. "Just saw Kathleen's

husband. Joey. That animal." With a quivering finger he pointed to a black SUV raising dust as it rocketed out of the lot. "Swore he'd kill me if I said anything in court. I can't testify."

"Nine-one-one," said the voice on my phone. "What's your emergency?"

Martin tried to stay upright by gripping the side mirror, but then his eyes closed. He slid down the side of my car and collapsed in the gravel.

"Just a minute," I told the dispatcher. Kneeling, I took the old man's pulse. Thready, erratic.

"My friend's having a heart attack."

"Where are you?"

"The big stone church near the park."

Stephen ran toward the front, looked at the sign, then trotted back. "St. Bartholomew Anglican."

"We'll be right there."

I put the phone back in my purse and sat next to Martin, holding his liver-spotted hand.

It was getting cold.

* * *

I stayed with Martin. Stephen looked down at the knit cap in his hand.

"Want this?" he asked.

I shook my head.

"May as well toss it," he said.

"Maybe the church has a rummage room. Where they sell used clothing."

He put the cap over his hand and used it like a puppet. "Put me out of my misery," he squeaked.

After finding a trash can at the edge of the parking

lot, he dropped the misbegotten creature in. "And to dust you shall return."

Martin's skin was getting colder. He still breathed, but shallowly.

Guests were starting to emerge from the reception. They looked shocked. The priest hurried over, his purple stole flapping in the breeze.

"Anything I can do?"

Before I could open my mouth, the cry of a siren answered his question. The sound grew louder, then died several yards away.

Two paramedics jumped out. The first, a twentyish man with a beard, tested Martin's neck with his fingers. After wrapping a blood pressure cuff around the patient's upper arm, he inflated it. As the air hissed out, he frowned.

The other, a short woman with biceps like Jillian Michaels, pushed a gurney toward us with one hand.

"Blood pressure's sixty over forty," the bearded one told her. He turned to me. "Know whether he's on any medications?"

"Takes pills. Probably nitroglycerin. Didn't have any with him this time."

Gently they lifted him onto the stretcher and loaded him into the ambulance. "You can follow us if you want," the woman said, climbing in the back. "We'll be taking him to NewYork-Presbyterian."

She slammed the door. The siren howled again.

Stephen poked his phone. "About twenty-five minutes, depending on traffic."

He was ten minutes too optimistic. I prayed the whole way.

Finally we sat in a third-floor waiting room, across from an elderly woman reading *WebMD Magazine*. A janitor polished the floor with one of those miniature Zamboni things.

"Hope he'll be okay," Stephen said, eyeing a distant vending machine.

"Wonder how old he really is," I said. "Got to be at least eighty."

We sat there, staring at the magazine. The cover story was about herpes. I missed C. Everett Koop.

Footsteps approached. Turning, I saw a woman in blue scrubs with a gray ponytail and a clipboard.

"I'm Dr. Bailey. Are you here with Mr. Curry?"

"Yes."

"He's definitely had a heart attack. Worn out, but I think he's going to make it."

"Can we talk with him?"

"I'm afraid not. He's asleep in the ICU. Maybe tomorrow. Visiting hours start at nine." With a weary sigh she headed down the hall.

Stretching, I groaned. "Let's go."

Stephen stood up. "Right after I get one of those Snickers. I'm hangry and unsatisfied."

"You know, Hunter's not going to be happy that Martin's backed down. He'll want us to come up with Plan B and leave Gina's case to her lawyer."

He shrugged. "So we won't tell him. Unless he asks."

I wobbled to my feet. "Does that machine have Twizzlers?"

He squinted. "Will Red Vines do?"

"If necessary."

Picking up my purse, I took out a couple of dollar bills and followed.

* * *

"So this is a police gym," I told Stephen the next day.

We were hanging around just inside the front door. The air smelled like liniment and wet towels. Wasn't sure what liniment was, much less what it smelled like, but it sounded like something Norman Mailer would write about.

I'd seen the dimly lit Rocky-training places in the movies, with faded boxing match posters on the walls and uppercut punching bags being hammered by angry fighters with cauliflower ears. This was more like Tone House on East 31st Street, or so I imagined. Working out took as much of my time as churning butter.

There were half a dozen cops in the place, maybe two of them in decent shape. The rest looked like the union had lost an argument over the definition of Fitness for Duty.

"See anybody who looks like Elaine Jeong?" I whispered.

Stephen pointed at a little group wearing white karate outfits with matching belts. Only one of the belts was black. "That woman seems to be in charge."

"Call me *sensei,*" she barked. "Means *teacher*. We all clear on that?"

The two muscle guys nodded. The rest rolled their eyes or nudged each other with their elbows.

"Don't recognize the voice," I said. "But then she's giving orders, not mumbling in an alley."

"Marshmallow man," said the woman, pointing at one of the skeptics. "A bad guy has you backed against a chain link fence. Your partner's been shot. The perp's grabbed your gun. What do you do?"

The Pillsbury Doughboy shrugged. "Take early retirement?"

One of the other underachievers laughed. The *sensei* didn't.

"Try to take me down," she challenged.

The Flabby One charged her, his right shoulder lowered like a battering ram. What happened next was a blur. A yell and a shriek, an involuntary somersault, a thud and a grunt and the victim's right arm bent behind his back.

"You can do better," the instructor said. "Not yet, but after a month or so of practice."

All he could do was writhe and moan.

"Who's next?"

Nobody volunteered.

"Take a break," *sensei* said. "Back in five minutes."

One of the Hans and Franz pumper-uppers helped the girly-man stand.

"Let's have that little talk," I said.

Stephen shuddered. "She looks pretty lethal."

I took him by the wrist. "Just don't make any sudden moves."

Slowly we moved forward. She was looking up at the lights with the wire grids on them, hands on hips.

"Elaine Jeong?" I asked.

Glancing up, she seemed for a moment to recognize us. But it passed as quickly as Dale Earnhardt soaring past the flag at the Indianapolis 500.

I made the usual introductions.

"I've gone over everything with the police," she said.

"Where were you when we got mugged?"

"Too bad about that. Detective told me when it happened. I was in my apartment, soaking a pulled hamstring in Epsom salts." The look she gave me would have frozen a flaming can of Sterno.

Her students were drifting back. The injured one sat

on a steel folding chair next to the ring, gingerly touching his arm.

She pointed at Hans. "Let's try that again." Even he seemed a little cowed.

"Nice to run into you again," I said. She pretended not to hear me.

The sounds of punching and weights knocking the floor receded behind us as we exited. I held the door open as Stephen, absorbed in poking his phone, walked with his head down.

"Huh," he said.

"Huh what?"

"Dr. Oz says Epsom salts aren't a treatment for pulled hamstring. Ice and compression bandages are."

"Detective Spiner would say that doesn't prove anything. But now I can't help wondering whether we can believe anything the *sensei* says."

CHAPTER 9

Back at NewYork-Presbyterian, we signed in as visitors and slapped on our stickers.

"Here to see Martin Curry," I said.

A pink-vested volunteer at the desk consulted a list. "Third floor. Check at the nurses' station for the room number."

The elevator swayed slightly as we ascended. "Hope he's awake," I said.

Stephen yawned. "Is it me, or does it seem like we've been up since about four o'clock?"

"Must wear you out seeing all those law enforcement types shoving each other around. Makes me tired trying to crowbar a straight answer out of Ms. Jeong."

The door slid open. Two nurses sat at their station. One was plucking Cheetos from a bag, the other glowered at her computer.

I leaned over the counter and smiled at the Frito-Lay fan. "Looking for Martin Curry."

After eyeing our stickers, she brushed orange dust from her fingers and glanced at her screen. "Room 323."

We followed the numbers, which took us down the hallway. A housekeeper wearing a mask stuck cartons of rubber gloves in dispensers next to the doors. "Wish I'd brought flowers or something," I whispered.

"He doesn't seem like a flowers kind of guy. Maybe a box of exploding cigars."

I knocked on 323 and nudged the door open. The TV was tuned to some closed-circuit channel that showed the day's menu. Nothing looked edible.

Martin was propped up in bed, nursing a big plastic cup of something orange. He bent in our direction and smiled weakly.

"Well, look who's here. Care for a taste of my breakfast?"

"What is it?" Stephen asked.

"Like Tang, but without that natural orange flavor. I'm practicing to be an astronaut. The doctors say I've got the lungs of Neil Armstrong, who's dead, and the fingers to pick up a very small moon rock."

"And the heart of a champion," I said.

"A champion hamster, maybe."

I rested my hand on the rail at the bottom of the bed. "What's your prognosis?"

He set the cup down. "To paraphrase Henny Youngman, the doctor gave me six months to live. I told him I'd couldn't pay my bill, so he gave me another six months."

"Good one."

He picked up the remote and shut down the TV. "I've been thinking about the Rosenthal situation. I just can't testify against Kathleen's ex-husband. Too old for the plastic surgery to hide my identity. Not to mention too handsome." He sank back in the bed. "Don't hate me."

"I couldn't. Who could hate the funniest man since Calvin Coolidge?"

He shook his head. "Silent Cal got a bum rap. Told him he'd win a second term if he'd just lighten up. But did he listen? No."

All at once the *1812 Overture* rang from my purse. It was Hunter.

"Carolyn, where are you?"

"In the hospital."

There was a pause. "What is it this time? You've been shot? Or shot somebody else, and you're apologizing? I can't afford to—"

"We're visiting Martin Curry. Heart attack, but still ticking."

"Thank whoever. We need him to testify."

"He's changed his mind. Near-death experiences will do that."

I could almost see the veins swelling in his neck.

"You've got a week to fix this. Waste as much time as you want playing detective, but only if you want to give up editing for good." The line went dead.

Martin raised an eyebrow. "How did he take it?"

"About the way you'd expect."

He sighed. "It's my fault."

"No, it's some nanny's fault for dropping him on his head."

* * *

In the lobby we sat down on a bench and pulled off our VISITOR stickers. I took out my phone.

"Who you calling?" Stephen asked.

"Spiner. She promised to look into the case where Roger supposedly bribed a juror."

No answer. Her voicemail was full.

"Gina should know what it was about," Stephen said.

I checked my watch. "At the jail it's after visiting hours. But I bet her lawyer's up to speed. Alexander Washington."

"I'll look up his address."

It was on Wall Street, near the East River.

"Location, location, location," Stephen said, putting his phone away. "His clients must pay through the nose, for an office in that neighborhood."

"Gina can't afford that. Wonder how they hooked up."

"Maybe he does pro bono, like Roger."

It took less time to get there than it did to find a parking space. The place was a stone's throw from One World Trade Center, a walkup no wider than a Winnebago.

"Not exactly Wachtell, Lipton, Rosen, and Katz," I said.

Stephen pushed the door open. "Not even Dewey, Cheatem, and Howe."

There must have been an elevator somewhere, but we couldn't find it. The steps were narrow and steep. At the top was a short hallway with glass and chrome doors. Stephen bent to drink from the water fountain, but it didn't work.

Alexander Washington didn't appear to have a receptionist. But the door to his inner sanctum was ajar, so I knocked.

"That you, Betty?"

"No," I said, stepping inside.

He was a head taller than Stephen, African American, with a white shirt whose sleeves were rolled up to the elbows. His suspenders were rainbows, though his girth probably made them unnecessary.

Standing behind a mountain of papers, he stuck his

thumbs under his braces. "Betty brings me the mail," he said.

I went through the usual introductions. "We're friends of Gina Casebeer."

"Ah, Pendleton House. I've known Gina since law school."

"Didn't I read something about you defending somebody famous about twenty years ago?"

He nodded. "The Reverend Hopkins Albert. Televangelist."

"Charged with fraud," Stephen said, not bothering to hide his glee. "Time shares in Montana that turned out to be only blueprints."

"My little claim to fame," Washington said. "Too bad the jury wasn't more merciful. He's still making license plates."

"So here's the deal," I said. "Gina told us Roger Trumbull was accused of jury tampering, but we don't know the details."

He opened a leather briefcase on his desk and dropped in a handful of work. "I'm on my way to a deposition, but for Gina, I'll squeeze you in." After snapping the valise shut, he tossed it on the sofa behind us and perched on the edge of his desk. Hard to imagine such an energetic fellow representing the dispirited Gina, but I assumed he had her best interests at heart.

"It was—what, about twelve years ago? Before Roger worked at Pendleton House. Corporate lawyer. Trinity Chemical was the target of a class action suit filed in Pennsylvania. Nineteen or twenty people had developed mesothelioma, allegedly from asbestos."

"Some still are," Stephen said. "Seen those commercials on TV?"

"Trinity hired a private detective to keep an eye on

Roger. The guy got a blurry photo of what might have been Roger having lunch with a juror, handing her an envelope. The charge was baseless. We showed he was at a company picnic that day. Juror died a year ago. Not mesothelioma. Natural causes."

After grabbing the briefcase, he wriggled into his sports jacket and straightened his tie.

"So why did Elaine Jeong threaten to expose him?" I asked.

He shrugged. "Don't know. But I'd love to ask her on the witness stand."

* * *

There was just enough left of the workday to get a few hours' work done. Or get into more trouble.

Avoiding Hunter's office, we went to our cubicles and hunkered down. My voicemail was full. I fielded urgent requests for optional things, like a silent fundraising auction for talkaholic mimes and two agents who pitched me the same project with different titles.

My assistant was nowhere to be found, not that it mattered. Anything more complex than shaking a half-empty toner cartridge was beyond her.

Several calls, texts, emails, and insincere apologies later, I called Stephen.

"You ready to go? Lord knows *I* am."

"I'm in the middle of watching a *Hiking with Kevin* video. On YouTube. He and John Grisham are walking the Appalachian Trail."

"Kevin who?"

"Nealon. Used to be on *Saturday Night Live*."

"Haven't watched since the year Billy Crystal was on. Anyway, I'm outta here."

"Give me five minutes."

Six minutes later I sneaked up behind him. He was watching a clip of a half-dozen owls in somebody's kitchen. Why anybody would keep them as pets was beyond me. Lifting a Justice League ruler from his desk, I proceeded to tap his head lightly.

"Hey, don't do that," he groused, smoothing his hair with his palm.

"Race you to the elevator."

"How come you're in such a hurry?"

"Been a long day."

He shut off his desk lamp. We headed for the hallway. I pushed the DOWN button with my thumb.

We sank to the first floor, then stopped. The doors rolled open.

There stood Joey Rosenthal, smiling, eyes wide with something between wonder and madness. He looked like he hadn't shaved in a week.

Stepping inside, he chuckled. "Fancy meeting you here."

"Oh, crap," Stephen mumbled.

I felt in my purse for the pepper spray. All I could find was lipstick.

The doors slid closed. He pushed the silver button to keep us from moving.

I backed against the wall.

"What do you want?" I asked, trying not to hyperventilate.

He scratched his chin. "How's *unconditional surrender* sound?"

CHAPTER 10

"UNDERSTAND YOU'VE BEEN LOOKING FOR ME," JOEY SAID.

I stared at the DOOR CLOSE button, wishing I could reach the one that said ALARM.

Something was wrong. Why wasn't he growling? Except for that twitch in his right eyelid, he seemed almost reasonable.

"Let's make a deal," he said, blocking the control panel with his hand. "If you'll quit trying to make me out as some kind of wife-beater, I won't take the gun from my pocket and leave your brains on the wall."

Stephen sank to the floor. At first I thought he was fainting, but he just got down on one knee.

"Sounds good," he said, doing the first involuntary millennial Don Knotts impression I'd ever heard. "You want that in writing?"

"Stop groveling," I whispered.

Joey laughed. "Can you do Bobcat Goldthwaite? He was a riot."

Taking hold of Stephen's arm, I pulled him up. "Mr.

Rosenthal, if you're innocent, why did Kathleen divorce you?"

His hand drifted toward his pocket but rose to massage the back of his neck instead. "Irreconcilable differences. She wanted Alan Alda; I wanted Angelina Jolie. We both struck out." He didn't exactly seem paralyzed with regret.

Stephen patted his pockets. "About that written agreement. You got a pen?"

Ignoring him, I studied the ceiling. "Nobody's willing to testify since you gave Martin Curry a heart attack."

Joey shook his head. "Not my fault. The old man hasn't taken care of himself." He paused. "Any further questions, Your Honor?"

"Under the circumstances, no."

Grinning, he pushed the OPEN button.

"Let's keep in touch," he said, tipped an invisible cap, and disappeared.

* * *

The door began to close. I held it open as Stephen stumbled out.

Eyes wide, he surveyed the lobby.

"Still here?" I asked.

"Don't see him."

I stepped out of the lift. "Can't afford to get too close. What a psycho."

* * *

We sat on a bench flanked by giant aloe plants. My back throbbed.

An elderly security guard sat next to the desk, staring

intently at his cell phone. White hair brushed back, big orange glasses. Obviously a big help when it came to taking down homicidal maniacs.

Stephen glanced to his right. "This reminds me of *Between Two Ferns,* the Zach Galifianakis thing."

"What's *that?*"

"Funny thing on the Internet."

"Sounds like a gardening show."

"You've seen *Murder on the Orient Express,* right?"

"Of course. The one with Albert Finney."

"No, the one where Kenneth Branagh has a mustache the size of a steer's longhorns."

"Didn't see it. And I think longhorns are a *kind* of steer, not the bony protrusions themselves."

"Anyway, it doesn't matter. The point is that *everybody* did it. They all took a stab at Ratchett, who was actually Lenfranco Cassetti."

"Played by Richard Widmark," I said.

"Johnny Depp in my version."

"Agatha Christie could get away with that. But in real life you couldn't get all those people to cooperate, much less take turns." I paused. "Reminds me more of *Clue.*"

"The movie or the game?"

"There was a movie?"

"Of course. Martin Mull, Tim Curry, Lesley Ann Warren . . ."

I shifted on the bench, trying in vain to find a tolerable position. "I remember playing the game at junior high sleepovers. All those rooms, lots of colors, the little plastic lead pipe in the library. Professor Plum. Mrs. Peacock . . ."

"I don't see the similarity. One's entertaining. The other's just moving little metal pieces on a board."

I looked at my watch and got up. "Probably safe to go

to our cars now. Besides, my spinal column is disintegrating."

I waved at the guard, but he was glued to his smartphone. Probably looking up dating prospects on SilverSingles.

Just in case, I rummaged through my purse again. This time I found the lipstick *and* the pepper spray.

* * *

Next morning I got a call from Alexander Washington. There were announcements about Delta flights in the background.

"About to catch a plane to Chicago. I've been considering some kind of plea bargain for Gina, but don't really want to go that route."

"*Plea* bargain? She's *innocent*."

"I'm convinced of that, too. That's not the reason I called, though."

The announcements got louder. I could barely hear him.

"She's been moved to a different cell!" he said, nearly shouting. "Her new roommate has threatened to kill her in her sleep."

CHAPTER 11

WE GOT IN THE CAR.

"Wish I had a 'Get Out of Jail Free' card," I said, starting the engine.

"What are you thinking? We'll convince them to move her to a different cell? Are you tight with the warden?"

"Of course not. But we've got to do *something*. At least see how she's doing."

It took 45 minutes to reach the visitor's lot at The Metropolitan Correctional Center. They confiscated the usual stuff at the front desk.

A different guard brought Gina down this time, joining the one who was already there. Our friend looked worse than ever, her eyes bloodshot behind her red glasses.

We picked up our phones. "Heard you got a new roommate," I said.

She nodded.

"Your lawyer told us she's sort of anti-social."

"You might put it that way."

"Are you okay?"

She tried to smile. "Never better."

"What can we do? Other than bringing you a file in a birthday cake."

"Green tea. It's what I miss most, besides safety and the freedom to take a bath."

Stephen leaned in my direction. "Probably contraband. The guards might mistake it for marijuana."

"I'm no pot expert, but I know my herbs. Those two are totally different."

I turned to Gina. "I remember the commissary at the Seattle County Jail. Outsiders could put money into an inmate's account. Must be a little store like that here. Maybe it's got some kind of tea. We'll make a deposit on the way out."

She nodded again. Her eyelids were starting to droop.

"Trying to avoid a suit over the book's hit a snag, but we're more worried about you. What with your homicidal roommate."

"Not anymore. They took her away and gave me an anarchist."

"Well, that's a relief."

"She snores. But I only notice when I'm awake. Which is less and less these days."

Suddenly an alarm went off. Not clangy, but the kind you might hear in a World War II movie during the London Blitz.

Stephen stood up. "What the—"

The sound of giant doors closing echoed like the slam of a bank vault.

The guards shouldered their weapons and looked around.

"Lockdown," one said.

The other cursed and put his finger on the trigger.

No longer sleepy, Gina shook herself. "What are we supposed to do?"

The siren was giving me an earache. "Don't know."

Stephen sniffed. "You smell smoke?"

The guards looked at each other. This time they both swore.

* * *

The siren stopped. The ringing in my ears didn't.

Somewhere a loudspeaker crackled to life. "Inmates will return to their cells immediately. Visitors must shelter in place."

Gina's guard stepped forward and took her elbow. "Come with me."

Shaking, she got to her feet.

"Tea," I said. "I'll remember." The guard led her away.

I stood up next to Stephen. We weren't the only visitors. A panicky woman with a cane and two men wearing clerical collars sat at a couple of tables.

"What do you think's going on?" the woman asked the remaining guard.

Silence.

One of the clerics turned to the woman and assured her things would be fine. "This isn't that unusual," the older one said.

"Except for the smoke," the other added. "Could be a riot."

The guard pointed his gun at the floor. "We don't use that word around here."

"Wish I had my phone," Stephen said. "Somebody might already be covering it."

I coughed. The smoke was getting worse. "Wonder

whether Gina's new cellmate might have something to do with this. You know how those anarchists are."

"Maybe it's just a fight."

"With a *fire?*"

The woman with the cane gripped the edge of her table and pushed herself to her feet. "How long do we have to stay here? I'm diabetic. Need my insulin."

The older minister got up and put his hand on her shoulder. "Shouldn't be long before things get back to—"

With a *WHOOOMP!* the wall exploded. Glass shattered. Charcoal gray smoke poured into the room.

A tattooed woman in an orange jumpsuit emerged from the hole in the wall like an avenging dark angel, revolver in hand. The guard whirled to face her, but she was quicker. Her gun flashed; he dropped. She stole his rifle.

Turning toward us, she yelled. "On the floor!" Backing into a corner, she swung the gun back and forth.

The woman with the cane whimpered. The clerics raised their hands, more in submission than prayer.

I prayed but didn't raise anything.

The inmate fired into the ceiling.

"Consider that a warning shot," she said.

* * *

Another explosion rocked the place, but more distant.

The woman shot out a window, apparently trying to let the smoke escape.

The siren cranked up again. So did my earache.

"Stay down," she commanded. "Gonna be here for a while."

I coughed. "The guard needs help."

"Lady, don't we all."

I pointed at the woman with the cane. "At least let her go."

The would-be guerrilla shook her head. "Not safe. Not for me, or her either."

Stephen waved his arms in frustration. "Are you trying to escape, or what? If you've got a list of grievances, maybe I could—"

"Shut up. If I want a hostage negotiator, I'll ask for one."

One of the phones on the wall rang.

"Speak of the devil," she said.

CHAPTER 12

THE SHOOTER PICKED UP THE PHONE AND LISTENED, THEN delivered a blistering barrage of blasphemy. Pressing the receiver against her chest, she looked at me.

"Are you Carolyn Norville?"

"Neville." No point in pretending. Eventually she'd get around to checking my driver's license.

"It's for you," she said.

Clearing my throat, I sat in a visitor's chair and took the phone. "Yes?"

"This is Gina Casebeer's new roommate."

"The anarchist? Never met one before. What's your name?"

"Joan of Arc."

"I take it that's a pseudonym."

"Brilliant deduction. Now shut up and quit trying to be a comedian."

I swallowed. "Is Gina okay?"

"There's a very sharp implement pointed at her throat."

"A knife."

"It is now. Used to be razor blades and a toothbrush."

"What do you want from me?"

"Your friend here says you can be trusted."

"I'd like to think so. But before we go further, I need to hear she's all right."

She grunted. "Hold on."

"Carolyn?" Gina was wheezing.

"You sound awful," I said.

"It's the smoke. And I think I smell tear gas filtering in from the other end of the cellblock. Smells like vinegar."

"Are you hurt?"

"Not yet. Just . . . well, you know. Tired."

"I would be too."

"Three women—a guard and two inmates—aren't so lucky. They're lying outside the cell across the corridor. Don't know what happened. Can't tell if they're alive."

The shooter grabbed the phone back, hung it on the hook, and poked me in the chest. "We have a list of non-negotiables." She counted them off on her fingers. "Everybody pulls back—SWAT team, guards, everybody. Open the cells. There are six of us. Need a helicopter to land in the yard, with safe passage to Cuba. Think you can manage that?"

I couldn't help laughing. "You're kidding, right? I'm an editor, not a—"

She fired the rifle into the ceiling. I flinched. "Today, you're a negotiator."

I thought of all the contracts I'd wrangled over with agents. Not exactly the same.

My eyes watered from the smoke. The guard was bleeding. The woman with the cane slumped over the table. The religious guys looked like they wanted to edge their way toward the window but didn't have enough faith.

I was in no position to argue.

* * *

"Isn't the FBI supposed to be in on this?" I asked. "Never met the warden. Haven't got a helicopter. The State Department doesn't know me from Adam."

"Of *course* you don't. You're a go-between. If they get me on the line, they'll waste time trying to psych me out while they surround this block. Now hang up and call the FBI. Here's the number."

After sending up a quick prayer, I dialed.

"You've reached the Federal Bureau of Investigation. For English, press one. *Para Español, presiona dos.*" It went like that for the next ten minutes or so as I tried to climb the world's tallest phone tree. Finally I got a real person.

"Agent Barnes," said a man's voice. I could barely hear him over the noise in the background.

"My name's Carolyn Neville. I'm being held at gunpoint in the visitor's room at The Metropolitan Correctional Center. We're in the middle of—"

"I know. I'm standing outside the wall. We've been here for about half an hour."

"Oh." I felt better. A little.

"I'm not really a negotiator. Just in the wrong place at the wrong time."

"Take a deep breath. Let's see what we can work out."

"They have a list of demands." I told him what they were.

"Sounds pretty typical," he said. "Way over the top. Maybe we can talk them down."

I looked at my captor. She wasn't smiling, and still had the gun.

"I feel a certain *urgency*," I whispered.

"Believe me, I sympathize. But it'll take time to arrange for a chopper, let alone one that can make it to Havana. Not even sure Cuba will take them in."

I coughed again. There was a long pause.

"Try to stall her," the agent said. "I'll get back to you."

He hung up.

* * *

"What did he say?" the shooter asked.

"Very sympathetic. And he'll work on it."

"Those guys are a joke. But they'll cave."

I proceeded to employ my considerable stalling skills.

"What'll you do if you get to Cuba?"

"Lie on the beach and eat a sandwich. Drink a *cerveza*. Maybe get a job rolling cigars. Definitely smoke a few."

The guard lying in the corner groaned.

The woman whirled and pointed her rifle.

"Just let me see how much he's bleeding and—"

She stared over my shoulder. "Hey! You reverends stay away from the window! Check the screw."

They looked around, confused.

"The *guard*," she said. "God, you're hopeless."

I backed away. "Can I take the diabetic lady's pulse?"

"Whatever."

It was weak, but regular.

The shooter walked over, finger on the trigger. "Reminds me of my mother. And I don't mean in a good way."

I turned toward Stephen. Staring at the gun, he

started to inch in the shooter's direction. I mouthed a *no* and shook my head.

He sat back down, pouting.

The phone rang. I sprinted toward it.

Agent Barnes answered.

"Get away from the windows," he warned. "And I mean *now*."

CHAPTER 13

I HESITATED. IF I MOVED, WHAT WOULD THE SHOOTER DO?

Deciding to chance it, I grabbed Stephen's arm and dashed to the table.

"Dive underneath," I whispered. "Something's about to happen."

"How do you know?"

"A little FBI agent told me."

Before we could get there, a *BOOM* thundered somewhere between the wall and the razor wire.

"Holy crap!" Stephen cried.

The old lady lifted her head for a second, but it sank back on her forearm.

The fluorescent lights flickered and so did the vending machine. I could still see well enough to notice more smoke filtering in from outside.

Something enormous was coming. The sound reminded me of a tank, kind of a squeaky rumble. Not that I'd heard any except in the movies.

The lady with the rifle raised it and shot out an overhead fixture. Screaming curses, she searched for a escape route but didn't find any.

With a *BAM* and a raining of concrete blocks, the blade of what looked like an army green snowplow smashed through the wall.

Stephen's mouth opened and closed like a bluegill's in the hull of a boat. Finally he spoke. "Hope it's on *our* side."

When the smoke had half cleared, there sat an armored vehicle twice the size of O.J. Simpson's fabled Bronco, coated with dust.

* * *

Four soldiers in khaki uniforms and helmets streamed like locusts from the hatch, assault weapons drawn.

"Cavalry's here," Stephen said.

"Military *and* FBI," I replied.

More soldiers followed.

A bit late, the ministers dove under the table. So did Stephen.

I watched as the red-faced shooter screamed. Outgunned, she dropped her weapon.

The phone rang again.

"Agent Barnes."

"We're alive," I said. "But we need an ambulance."

"Already here. We've secured the perimeter on all sides."

He didn't say anything about casualties.

I dragged Stephen out from under the table. He brushed dust off his jeans.

"Wonder what's happened to Gina," I said.

I knelt by the guard. Still alive, but just barely.

Barnes climbed through the gaping hole in the wall,

coughing. After kicking away the rifle, he cuffed our former captor.

Two paramedics ran in with a stretcher and carried the guard away.

The ministers crawled out and tried to rouse the lady with the cane. She didn't budge. Supporting her shins and shoulders, they moved her to safety.

I stood there, dizzy, too tired to care how much I resembled a chimney sweep.

As Barnes led the shooter away, she regarded me sadly.

"Guess that *cerveza* will have to wait," she said.

* * *

Another guy in a blue FBI vest passed by me, using some kind of metal detector.

"Looking for leftover bombs?" I asked.

"Can't confirm or deny it," he said.

"Got a friend who's an inmate. Being held at gunpoint by one of the rioters. Can you help me find out whether she's okay?"

Sighing, he set down the detector. "Which cellblock's she in?"

I did my best to remember. "Three West. About six percent sure."

He detached a walkie-talkie from his belt and finally got through. "What's your friend's name?"

"Casebeer. Gina."

After a brief conversation, he turned to me. "Wrong cellblock."

He put the device back to his ear. "Can I talk to a guard?"

There was a long pause, then some muttering I couldn't decipher.

"Thanks," the agent said, and switched the walkie-talkie off.

"She's been stabbed, but just superficially. The girl with the gun was shot when another armored vehicle broke down the wall on that side."

"Can I talk to Gina?"

"Been taken to the infirmary."

CHAPTER 14

STEPHEN AND I CRUNCHED OUR WAY THROUGH THE DEBRIS. Tired of coughing, I found a sink in the visitors' room. There were plastic cups in the cabinet. I took one and turned the faucet handle. Nothing came out.

"Probably blew up some pipe," he said.

After finding two dollars in my purse I tried the vending machine. The Tropicana lemonade seemed promising. Inserting the bills with Washington's head up, I waited. There was a buzz, but George didn't move. When I attempted to pull him out, he resisted. I gave up.

"I could pound on the side," Stephen offered. "Sometimes it works."

"Not in front of the FBI, okay?"

Wishing I had a canteen, I shifted toward the man in blue. "Can we visit the infirmary?"

"You'll have to ask somebody who works for the jail, but I doubt it." His cellphone rang. He listened. "Be right there," he said, and put it back in his pocket. "They want me outside. Media's starting to show up. Sure hope

Barnes does the briefing. Those people are a pack of jackals." He paused. "Good luck getting to your friend."

The ministers picked their way back through the gap in the wall. They were sweating too. I resisted the urge to beg for a cup of living water.

"How's the diabetic lady?" I asked.

The older one wiped his forehead with the back of his hand. "Paramedic said she's close to a coma, but she's likely to make it."

"I've got a friend in the infirmary. Can you help me see her?"

The younger one tried the tap, then sighed when it yielded a single drop. "Visitors aren't allowed." He nodded toward his colleague. "We can get in if the patient's in critical condition. Want us to check on her? While we're at it, maybe we can get a drink."

"Be great if you could bring us some," Stephen said.

"If not, we'll find a rock you can strike with your staff."

"Huh?"

"Like Moses in the desert."

"Oh, yeah. The guy with the tablets."

"That's the one."

"I'd appreciate it."

The clerics looked at each other. "Don't toy with him," the older one said.

"Sorry."

The older one put a hand on Stephen's shoulder. "We'll try to get something. If you're here when we get back, we'll split it with you."

Going to the table, he retrieved their phones. "See you later."

The old Samsung rang from my purse. It was Hunter. I put him on speaker.

"Where *are* you?"

"In the middle of a prison riot. Well, more of an aftermath."

"God, are you kidding? The thing's all over the news."

I gave him the *Reader's Digest* version. He didn't believe me.

"Why would they ask *you* to negotiate? What are we paying *them* for?"

"You'd have to ask Joan of Arc."

"Who?"

"Never mind."

"Well, get out of there and come to the office. You still have less than a week to resolve the issue with the book."

"If I don't, it'd make you look bad."

"Never entered my mind."

Stephen opened his mouth, stuck in his finger, and made a gagging sound. I was pretty sure it had nothing to do with thirst.

* * *

We decided not to make our grand exit through the hole in the wall. Instead, we took the official route through the reception area and front door.

Nothing could have prepared us for the sea of reporters, microphones, remote broadcast trucks, and law enforcers that met us when we emerged. Every news outlet in the state had to be there. Rank upon rank they stood like a secular choir, back rows obscured by the smoke. Armored vehicles and soldiers were retreating.

"Looks like they're wrapping up a press conference," Stephen said. An NYPD officer who looked like Anderson Cooper was taking questions.

"How many casualties so far?" yelled a woman I recognized, but couldn't remember which brand of Eyewitness News she worked for.

"Don't have the numbers yet. We do know at least three people have died."

"Inmates or rioters?"

"Can't comment."

Another newsperson, a diminutive bald fellow with a mustache that looked like two smears of brown shoe polish, waved. Must be a radio guy, I thought.

"Who negotiated with these domestic terrorists?" he demanded.

The officer hesitated. "I'm not sure. I suppose it was the FBI." He looked back to the front steps. "Anybody here from—"

"Right here!" said Stephen, waving. He bounded to the podium. The officer stepped aside, suspicion etched on his face.

"*You* were the negotiator?" he asked.

Stephen gripped the bully pulpit with both hands. "No, not me. I think I can, however, speak for the hostages. At least most of them." He introduced himself, carefully spelling his name.

Another Eyewitness News chick, her best side to the camera, called out. "Who's the real hero in all this?"

Putting a hand over his heart, Stephen lowered his head. "Certainly not *me*."

"Nobody suggested you are."

"I'll let time sort that out." He proceeded to tell his story, leaving out the part about hiding under the table.

By the time he was done a third of the reporters had drifted away. Lights were shut off, cameras packed in aluminum cases. Officer Cooper was consulting his watch.

"Let's take one more question."

The radio troll waved again. "We still haven't met the negotiator."

Stephen bowed in my direction. "She's standing right there. My friend and mentor, Carolyn Neville."

About 50 heads pivoted toward me. The silence was eerie.

"That's Carolyn with a *c* and an *lyn*," Stephen said. "And Neville with an *lle*. We're both from Pendleton House Publishing, right here in Manhattan."

He surrendered the pulpit. I installed myself, wishing I'd taken that Public Relations class in college.

A middle-aged woman with an admirably matronly figure and curly black hair put her microphone to her lips. A label on the side of her cameraman's Panasonic said WTNH-TV.

"Is it true this was all a 'death by cop' thing, that the kidnappers knew they'd never make it to Cuba?"

"I don't think so. The woman who held us was a real person who thought she had something to look forward to. She wanted a few simple things. Like freedom. One of the organizers had made her promises she couldn't keep."

"Some on the Internet are already suggesting this is an example of women's empowerment. Taking over the prison."

"I won't dignify that with an answer."

"Then maybe what *you* did is an example. You're a role model."

Before I could deny it, Stephen took the mike. "Any more questions for me?"

Silence reigned for about 30 seconds.

"Guess not," I whispered.

Taking his hand, I led him away, ignoring the Fourth Estate.

* * *

Next morning I woke in my condo, every muscle aching. At least I'd stopped wheezing.

Not feeling up to breakfast yet, I turned on the TV and channel-surfed, looking for news about the riot. Couldn't find anything. Should have been the top story.

For a moment I wondered whether I'd dreamed it all. My formerly white dress, which had died of smoke inhalation, was slung over a chair in the kitchen. Proof I hadn't made the thing up.

My phone rang. I went to the hall seat and fished it from my purse.

"Is this Carolyn Neville?" The voice wasn't familiar.

"I think so."

"Peter O'Dell from the *Today* show. I'm a producer."

I blinked.

"We saw you at the scene of the riot. You were great."

"If you say so." My stomach was starting to growl.

"Love to have you on the show. Do a segment or two."

"Far as I'm concerned, my fifteen minutes of fame are over. Thanks anyway."

"But—"

I hung up.

Scavenging for something to eat, I found a couple of stale chocolate donuts in the breadbox.

After brewing some coffee, I sat in front of the idiot box and stared at *The Flintstones,* chewing like a cow on cud.

I'd always considered myself more Wilma than Betty.

Wilma was no-nonsense, a little sarcastic, putting up with a club-wielding caveman posing as her boss.

My best friend Mikki was Betty, perky and energized and prone to giggling. Unlike Betty, though, Mikki stuck with one hair color.

I picked up my phone and got her voicemail.

"Hey, just wanted to check in. There was this murder, a guy at work, and this freak in an elevator who wanted to kill me. And maybe you heard about the prison riot. I was there, too, and some guy from the *Today* show—"

Out of breath, I stopped. The heck with it. What was the point? The story was too long, too complicated. And what did I want her to do?

"I'll leave that for next time we get together." Interrupting myself, I tried to think of a three-point landing. "Remember the first and last run we did in the park? I'm like that now. Running out of steam with a long road ahead. So I'll give you five bucks to pray for me. Call me back while I'm still able to pick up a phone."

CHAPTER 15

AFTER A SHOWER, I CALLED STEPHEN.

It rang and rang. Finally an irate voice broke in. "Do you know what time it is?"

"Yeah. Howdy Doody time."

"Too early to talk about things that happened before I was born. And I'm too sore to get out of bed."

"Mostly in the jawbone area, I imagine."

"Hey, somebody had to answer those questions. It's the people's right to know."

"Okay, look. We have to resolve the Kathleen Rosenthal case to get Hunter off our backs. Then we can concentrate on the murder."

"I have to go to the bathroom."

"Too much information. I'll find out when her show is tonight. Maybe we can get backstage beforehand. She wants this thing cleared up as much as we do."

"According to my bladder, time's up. Call me later."

An Internet check revealed Kathleen's current show was a revival of *Hello, Dolly*. The reviews were mostly positive, though the *Times* said she was no Midler, let alone Streisand or Channing. Most of the plaudits went to Lin-Manuel Miranda's Vandergelder and Harry Connick Junior's well-meaning stab at Louis Armstrong.

Curtain time was 8 p.m. Traffic was a mess, of course. At 7:00 we parked next to the Intrepid Sea, Air, and Space Museum and took a cab to the theater district. Striding like Gullivers, we hurried down the pedestrian mall, which was packed. Two unconvincingly costumed characters chose us as maypoles to dance around.

"Who are these guys supposed to be?" I asked, almost out of breath.

"Dr. Strange and Green Lantern. An unnatural wedding of the Marvel and DC universes."

"Comic books, I take it."

"And movies."

I checked my watch. "We've got forty-five minutes."

"How do we get to her dressing room? We don't have tickets."

I stopped under a deli's peppermint-striped awning and took out my phone. "She knows us." I found her number.

She picked up. "Yes?"

The crowd was so loud I practically had to yell. "Kathleen? Carolyn Neville. Two of us from Pendleton House are here. Can you give us five minutes?"

"I'm in makeup. Is it about the book?"

"We're trying to get things resolved."

"Yeah, okay. There's a tall guy in a red velvet suit to the right of the Will Call ticket booth. Have him give me a ring. I'll tell him to let you through."

I hung up. "Let's go."

The man in the velvet suit wore a top hat, making

him look like a stern Willy Wonka. Picking up a house phone he dialed, said a few words, then nodded.

"Take a right to the hallway, then about twelve doors down take a left at the AUTHORIZED PERSONNEL sign. The dressing rooms have name cards."

"Thanks."

Nobody stopped us. The further we went, the fewer we encountered. Finally we spotted Kathleen's door and knocked.

"It's unlocked." Her voice sounded strained.

It was what I expected—a room the size of my office, with a bulb-rimmed mirror and a vase full of yellow roses and three chairs.

Kathleen, in costume except for her hat, was applying the last of her eyeliner. She put the pencil down. "Things are a little chaotic. One of the minor players just broke his leg. Literally."

Stephen stepped forward. "I could take his place."

She smirked. "What was your name again?"

"Stephen Ames."

"An editor, right?"

"By day, yes."

"And by night?"

"Still an editor. But I've done a little acting."

"Think we've got it covered."

I tried not to let my mortification show. "We've got questions about Joey. First of all, what do you think he'll do if things don't go his way?"

"He's a big fan of beating me up. Probably kill me if he thought he could get away with it."

"Is there anybody in his life he listens to? Anybody sane who could rein him in?"

She thought for a moment. "His mom used to keep him in check, but she died three years ago."

"What's he do for a living?"

"Has a band. Which I can't stand. And the inheritance from importing."

"Where's the band practice?"

"In his garage. They might be there now." She ripped a page from a small pad on the vanity table and took up a pen. "Here's the address."

The door opened. A stagehand stuck his head in. "Curtain in seven minutes, Ms. Rosenthal."

"We're grateful for your time," I said. "Hear the show is a hit."

"The reviewers love Lin-Manuel. They hate me."

"Everybody's a critic," Stephen said.

She picked up her hat, a flowery, veil-wrapped example of the milliner's art the size of a dinghy. "Call me sometime. I can get you comp tickets."

"We'll do that," I said, "if we're still on the payroll."

"And breathing," Stephen added.

* * *

We could hear the din from outside Joey's house as we parked on the street. My eardrums begged me not to venture inside.

Knocking on the garage door, I got no response.

Ringing the doorbell didn't work either.

After waiting in vain for a break in the noise, I pounded on the garage door again.

Finally it rose like Kathleen's curtain probably had done half an hour ago, but not so quietly.

It took a few moments for my eyes to adjust to the light. The musicians were listening to their own music, not practicing. A cooler of beer cans sat between them.

Three ponytailed, balding guys who looked like the

Ungrateful Dead lounged around on director's chairs, pouring Coors down their gullets and belching. Joey talked on his cellphone, waving a fist in the air.

Taking one look at us, he frowned more deeply and stuffed the phone in the pocket of his blue puffer vest, probably from Eddie Bauer.

"What are *you* doing here?" he asked.

I manufactured a mechanical smile. "Pendleton House has a music division. They'd like copies of your band's CDs."

He snorted. "If they're trying to buy me off, they'd better be ready to pay the *big* money."

After gulping a Coors and burping like a fourth grader trying to impress his friends in the lunchroom, he rummaged around in an apple crate.

Stephen approached the Ungrateful Dead. "So, dudes, I'm Stephen Ames. Play a little guitar myself."

They leered at each other.

"A *little* guitar," said the one with the longest ponytail. "That'd be a *ukelele,* wouldn't it?"

They all laughed. The one wearing a Styx sweatshirt produced a spectacular belch. Twenty seconds at least.

"Ah," Rosenthal said, holding up three CDs in cases, no labels. He tossed them to me. I dropped one, but it didn't break.

"Perfect," I said. "They'll love these, I know it."

"So how did you find me? Kathleen?"

The mental image of him punching her kept me from answering.

Cursing, he grabbed a guitar from its stand and brandished it over his head as if eager to smash it on the cement.

"Hey, man!" cried the champion belcher. "Don't go all Pete Townshend on us. That one's *mine.* It's a *Fender.*"

Sulking, Joey put it back.

"Marry in haste," he said. "Divorce even hastier. Next time bring cash."

He got up and punched the garage door button. The curtain rose for Act Two.

* * *

I took my place behind the wheel.

"What good did *that* do?" Stephen asked. "And when did Pendleton House get into the music business?"

"Well, it's a small part of the company. Sheet music and instructional books. Never know when they'll get the urge to be the next Capitol Records."

"So you're *almost* being honest."

"If nothing else, it buys us time if Joey thinks he might get his big break and payoff without going to court."

I started my car and headed for Stephen's. We rode in silence.

"What was it Kathleen said about importing?" I asked when we reached his vehicle.

"That's how Joey's dad got rich."

I paused. "You know my friend Mikki, right?"

"The one with chameleon hair."

"Works at an import house. Wonder whether she's heard any rumors about Joey's father."

"So ask."

"Her bosses have always sounded like borderline crooks. If they could prove Joey's just as twisted, it could be harder for him to play the victim. Might back off to keep himself out of the papers."

"Probably wouldn't take kindly to blackmail and just get rid of us."

"Not if we manage to make it public before he gets the chance."

"Don't have a megaphone. Or a mouthpiece."

"Sure we do. We're media darlings, remember?"

CHAPTER 16

NEXT MORNING I CALLED MIKKI BEFORE WORK. HER BOSS hated it when she wasted time during office hours, doing frivolous things like leaving her desk to go to the bathroom.

"Carolyn! Got your message. This is the next time we talk, so go ahead. Start with the prison riot."

"I'll get to that. You probably know all about the Rosenthals."

"Our archenemies."

"You know Joey?"

"Never met him, but my boss thinks he's the devil incarnate."

"Joey's ex-wife wrote a book for us. Says he's an abuser. He's threatened to sue us."

"And kill you, right?"

"Right."

"It's always something, isn't it? Now get to the prison riot. If I'm five minutes late, they'll dock me fifty bucks."

"Don't you ever watch the news?"

"Not the depressing parts. I tend to stick with *TMZ* and *Entertainment Tonight*."

"Okay. My friend Gina's in prison, charged with murder. These anarchists wanted to go to Cuba, so they took some of us hostage. I ended up having to be a negotiator. Do FBI stuff."

"You're *kidding*."

"They were shorthanded that day."

"How'd you get out?"

"The Army plowed through the wall with a tank and some soldiers. You can look the rest up on the Internet."

"What's this about the *Today* show?"

"They wanted to interview me about the riot. I said no, but I might change my mind."

She made an exasperated noise. "If I had a chance to be on *Good Day New York*, let alone *Today*, I wouldn't think twice."

"I don't doubt it. Anyway, I have this idea. You can help us set a trap for Rosenthal."

"Does it involve guns or tanks?"

"Hopefully not. We need to find out whether his company has any skeletons in its closet. Maybe your boss knows something."

"If he doesn't, he'll make it up. He'd love to torpedo his biggest competitor."

"That's what I thought. Now, if—"

"He's no angel himself. I don't like the thought of having to bring this up, though. He's been trying to hit on me for years. Might assume I don't think of him as a rancid weasel anymore."

"You won't have to do it alone. I'll sit in on the conversation."

She laughed. "You know I love you, Carolyn. But what's in it for me?"

"Easy. You won't have to go looking for a new best friend when the guy kills me."

"On one condition."

"What?"

"Promise you'll give me a case of pepper spray for my next birthday. In case my boss gets the wrong idea."

* * *

That afternoon Mikki and I sat in the office of Darrell "Dub" Kratt, president of Icarus Imports. He was bald with a sandy fringe, at least 20 pounds overweight, stuffed into a greenish-blue suit that looked like it came from Big Lots. The indigo tie was embroidered with a gold pineapple. His smile was too white to not involve dentures.

His lair was decorated with tacky imports—a fisherman's net dotted with glass floats, Barbie ripoffs sporting orange hair and red lips looking like they'd been dabbed on by a chimp with a toothpick.

I'd never seen Mikki so conservatively dressed, gray and angular—enough to repel the most libidinous office sleazebag. Her new hairstyle was a modified Mohawk, like that girl in the *Sally Forth* comic strip I don't read. Only it was pink. Couldn't figure out how she got away with it at work. But she spent most of her time on the phone, and Dub's hope sprang eternal.

I let her handle the introductions.

He looked me up and down, flashed those choppers, and folded his hands on his desk. "Mikki's told me *so* much about you."

She turned to me and shook her head in silent refutation.

"Feel like I know you already, Ms. Neville," he added.

"And vice versa."

"I'm flattered."

I crossed my legs demurely. "Do you know much about the Rosenthals and their company?"

Leaning back in his chair, he whistled. "Now *there's* a question. Joe Senior looked innocent as a baby's butt, but deep down he was slippery as a fox."

His eloquence reminded me of Hunter. Perhaps it was some kind of executive malady.

"Joe would sell calculators and Whoopie cushions by the gross, then short every order by two or three dozen. Hardly anybody complained. If they did, Joe would cut off their credit."

"Shocking."

"That's just the beginning. He totally ignored all the Consumer Product and Safety Commission's defective toy recalls. Cat toys with feathers that fell out as soon as you opened the package. Little pinball machines with poisonous lead shot in them. Not to mention the Go Fish cards with nasty pictures on the back."

I took out my pad and started scribbling.

"Then there was the time, 1997, when Icarus outbid Rosenthal for the Ali Baba contract. Joe saw to it that there was a fire in our warehouse. Melted half a million dollars' worth of Chinese hard goods into a puddle of toxic glop. Nobody could prove it, of course."

"Bet you'd like to see Rosenthal held accountable."

"Honey, nothing would please me more."

I put the pad away. "All I need is Mikki for one day."

She looked worried.

He winked at her. "She's one indispensable lady. But I think we can work around it."

"How about tomorrow?"

"You got it."

When he shook my hand, I cringed. It felt like one of those slimy rubber snakes from the Dollar Store, undoubtedly a mainstay of his inventory.

* * *

After our meeting I called Stephen and told him how things had gone.

"Sounds like Kratt and Hunter are twins," he said.

"Or victims of the same disease."

"Speaking of Hunter, he wants us back in the office. Sales conference is coming up."

"Can you cover for me? Mikki and I have plans."

"I'm not going to face those hyenas alone."

"Just for a couple of days. Got another corporate giant to expose."

"You owe me one."

"I'll pay you in cryptocurrency."

"But—"

I hung up.

Next day Mikki and I parked at The Rosenthal Company. This time she was dressed to impress P.T. Barnum—Kelly green pantsuit with a rhinestone collar.

We sat in the lot. "Now, what are we trying to do again?" she asked.

"Our objective is to get into the CEO's office."

"Russell Barnes."

"We're looking for evidence of fraud, arson, or worse."

"What's worse than that?"

"Murder, I guess."

"I don't know much about computers. And I hate Excel."

"So do I. Don't know their passwords, either. We'll do the best we can."

The lobby was the opposite of the one at Icarus. Tasteful.

Barnes' admin was at the desk. She looked like fashion designer Edna E. Mode from *The Incredibles,* all in black with oversized glasses.

She eyed us with disdain. "Do you have an appointment?"

"Not exactly. But we have inside information about Icarus Imports that Mr. Barnes will be very interested in."

Mikki leaned forward. "I'm a disgruntled employee."

She stood up. "Very well. Wait here."

"So far so good," Mikki whispered.

The admin returned. "Right this way."

Barnes was the opposite of Kratt, meticulously dressed, businesslike, with a nose so sharp you could slice cucumbers with it. No cheap decorations blighted the wall. Just a series of framed Japanese calligraphies.

He stood up behind his desk, looking guarded. "I'm due at a meeting in fifteen minutes. What's this about?"

I did the introductions.

"Interesting. Have a seat."

"My colleague has some embarrassing information about your main competitor."

"I'm listening."

Mikki folded her hands in her lap. "Three years ago, Icarus Imports double-billed the State of New York for a quarter of a million dollars in plastic trophies, candy, and battery-powered fans. Used them for awards at employee banquets, that kind of stuff."

"Not exactly a federal crime."

"That's just the beginning. Last year my boss ordered

our chief of security to put a bug in your office. It's probably still here."

He straightened up. "Are you serious?"

"I swear."

He looked at his watch. "Got to get to that meeting."

"We'll be glad to sweep the room for the listening device while you're gone," I offered.

He hesitated. "Sure you know what you're doing? No offense, but you don't seem much like corporate spies to me."

"We're not. Think of us as lovers of justice."

He picked up his briefcase and walked toward the door. "I'll be back in thirty minutes or less."

Mikki was shaking but breathed a sigh of relief.

I closed the door behind him and locked it.

"*More* than thirty, I hope," I said.

CHAPTER 17

I RAISED BOTH ARMS AND BENT MY ELBOWS, FLAPPING them up and down like a Mayan priestess over a virgin sacrifice.

"What the heck are you doing?" Mikki asked.

"Pretending to sweep for bugs."

"Nobody's watching."

"I just like the feeling of power. *You* look for evidence."

She moved from one filing cabinet to another, unsuccessfully trying to pull out drawers. Only one opened.

"Am I supposed to look under Fraud, Arson, or Murder?"

"A little too obvious. Check spreadsheets for unexplained expenditures."

"Told you I hate Excel."

I patted her on the shoulder. "But you hate your boss more, right?"

"Can't. Have to love my neighbor. Overwhelming frustration and nausea might be forgivable."

Going to work, she riffled through folder after folder. "If I break a nail, you're paying for it."

"Think I don't know they're all fake?"

"You're just jealous. Since your boyfriend the lawyer died, you've bitten yours to the quick." She rolled a drawer shut. "I'm no accountant, but nothing looks that suspicious to me."

"Then try to find legal memos."

She resumed riffling. I went to the door and listened for possible interlopers.

"Just a lot of bills. And a Christmas card from the firm of Attenborough and Dunbar with a list of lawyer jokes."

"Look in the main desk drawer. See whether there's a key."

"Paper clips. Man, what a big eraser. Oh, wait." She held up a key and tossed it to me.

I tried it on the nearest cabinet, then another. "We've struck gold. Maybe."

After unlocking the rest, we started riffling in unison. In one credenza I found a brown accordion folder. No papers. It jangled when I shook it. More keys.

I dumped them on the desk. "See any safes or security boxes?"

"No, but those fortune cookie sayings on the wall might have something behind them."

Grabbing a handful of keys, I walked to the nearest calligraphy.

Suddenly the door opened. It was Barnes' admin.

She frowned over the rims of her glasses. "What do you think *you're* doing?"

* * *

"Do you have permission to ransack the place?" she demanded.

"Mr. Barnes said we could check for listening devices."

She gasped. "Industrial espionage?"

"Confidential, you understand."

"My lips won't sink ships." She turned and left.

Mikki and I looked at each other. "Close one," she said.

I took down the first frame. Nothing behind it but a very dead spider.

The second one took some prying. When if finally came off, I saw a gray metal plate with a keyhole. Took me nine tries to find its mate. Turning the key, I proceeded to open the box.

Another accordion folder was inside. In it was a batch of letters from Attenborough and Dunbar.

Among them was one advising Rosenthal to save money by settling out of court with the family of a child who'd swallowed a small rubber ball. It had blocked his airway, leading to brain damage.

I read it out loud. "'We recommend a sum of $150,000,'" it said.

Mikki slapped her hand on the desk. "I'm no lawyer, but—"

"I know. Easily worth a million."

"'If we wait,'" the letter continued, "'we might have to face a sympathetic jury.'"

"Wish they had," Mikki said.

I stuffed the letters in her my purse. "Wonder whether they settled." After rehanging the calligraphy and returning the keys to the drawer, I pointed toward the door.

We left just as Barnes came back. I nearly bumped

into him.

"Find anything?" he asked, his brow furrowed.

"No bugs," I said, and gave a thumbs-up. "We'll be in touch."

* * *

Congratulating ourselves for not being discovered, we drove to Mikki's place.

Things had changed since I'd last been there. The neon orange dinosaur in the corner had given way to a bust of Beethoven with a garland of grape leaves on his head.

Mikki brewed tea while I spread the letters across the coffee table.

"How are we going to get those back in the security box?" she asked.

"Don't have to."

I read another letter. It informed Rosenthal that Attenborough and Dunbar had hired an expert witness who'd testify that ingesting rubber could actually kill the human papilloma virus.

"Wow," Mikki says. "That's *low*."

We divvied up the rest. Most didn't look particularly incriminating.

The last one I scanned was signed by Dunbar himself, responding to questions about arson. Rosenthal seemed concerned that one of its competitors might try to burn down its property.

"'As for the question of whether you have sufficient insurance to cover the damage, I suggest you consult your agent,'" the attorney wrote.

"Not exactly a smoking gun," I said. "But it's a place to start."

CHAPTER 18

NEXT MORNING STEPHEN AND I MET IN THE PENDLETON House lunchroom. The place was empty except for a janitor sipping something at one of the tables. She was Rosie the Riveter, right down to the scarf on her head.

I told my senior editor about my brief career in industrial espionage, making sure to mention Mikki's mohawk.

"Oooh, that's a bold statement. Haven't seen one of those since Rihanna."

"And Pink. They look a lot alike."

He sipped his coffee. "So now we copy the letters and wave them in Rosenthal's face."

"I'd prefer to walk softly, not carry a big stick. Especially when a guy like Joey is holding the stick. First we should listen to Joey's CD to see whether Pendleton might be crazy enough to sign him up."

"Got a CD player in your office? I'm an mp3 man myself."

"Can't listen to music when I work. Distracts me. Let's try my car."

The first album was called *Vengeance Is Mine.* A black-and-white picture of a headless Nazi graced the cover.

"Somebody's been cutting and pasting stock photos," I said.

I pushed the disc into the slot and waited. All at once a slashing guitar chord came close to fracturing that little stirrup bone in my ear.

"*Jeez,*" Stephen cried, dialing down the volume. "I like loud music, but I'd like to be able to hear when I'm sixty-four."

A ragged scream bounced from the front windshield to the back. I turned it down further.

"Not exactly Huey Lewis and the News," I said, swallowing to make my ears pop.

"Can't hold a candle to Elvis Costello."

I hit the EJECT button. "Think we can agree on something, despite our wildly divergent musical tastes."

He nodded. "This sucks."

"No point in playing it into the phone for Hunter."

"Or sampling the other albums."

I slipped the disk back into its case. "Let's copy the letters. But we'll skip the big stick and just meet Mr. Rosenthal in a public place."

"The Statue of Liberty. Really dramatic."

"Not *that* public. And I got seasick on the Staten Island Ferry once."

"Empire State Building."

"Don't want to pay to ride to the top. Rockefeller Center's free, if we don't go in."

"On the steps, near the flags," he said.

"Fine. I'll call Joey."

Stephen looked at the remaining albums. One was *Spinal Crap.* I won't describe the illustration. The other was *Goodbye Kitty*. The little pink creature seemed to have lost her head.

I held up the first album.

"Seems to be a pattern here," he said.

"Let's hope we're not next."

* * *

A few phone calls later, everything was arranged. At 11 a.m. we met Joey at the designated spot.

He was solo, dressed in black, unaccompanied by the Boys in the Band. Couldn't help wondering whether he'd brought something lethal.

He sat on the top step and stretched out his legs, much to the irritation of employees and tourists. We stood, backs to the railing.

"Listened to the CDs?" he asked, examining his fingernails.

Stephen and I looked at each other.

"Got a good taste of them," I said. "Very . . . *impactful*."

Stephen nodded.

"Unfortunately, Pendleton seems to be going in a different creative direction. It's out of our hands."

"I'm sure you'll find your audience," Stephen said. "Start with dangerous loners."

Joey frowned. "Think that's funny?"

"It'd be a great name for your band. Classic, like Devo."

"The guys with flowerpots on their heads?"

"You don't have to wear those." He cleared his throat. "Just a suggestion."

"So you don't like my work. What's to keep me from suing you now?"

I took three letters from my purse. Probably not a

good time, but I doubted there'd be a better one. I handed them over.

The more he read, the more his face reddened. When he finished, the swearing began.

He stuffed the letters in his back pocket. His hand started to go under his jacket as if for a gun, but a glance at the crowd changed his mind.

"Hope somebody's got your back. When I come for you two, there won't be a warning. We'll be alone. I know where you live."

Tingling, I turned to go down the steps. My heel caught, and I felt myself falling forward. Stephen caught my elbow.

I didn't have to look back to know Joey was staring at me.

* * *

"What now?" Stephen asked.

I stopped. "Don't they do the *Today* show in Rockefeller Center?"

"Yeah, but this is a heckuva time to take the tour."

"I don't want a tour. I want an interview."

He laughed. "You can't just walk in and do that. You've got to get booked and everything. Besides, it's on in the *morning*."

"May I remind you I turned down an appearance on the show when the riot was over? If I can get on for that, maybe I can slip in some comments about The Rosenthal Company."

"Talk about bad publicity."

"If it goes public, Joey will be the first person the police look at if something happens to us."

"I feel much better now."

Turning, I faced the massive monolith of 30 Rock.

Joey was gone.

"Let's see if we can give them an exclusive," I said.

CHAPTER 19

I'd never had reason to go inside Rockefeller Center. I'd watched the Christmas tree lighting in 1996, when Michael Bolton and William Jefferson Clinton failed to get me into the holiday spirit. That was the year I gained ten pounds eating Paul Newman's fat-free fig newtons.

Everything was gold inside, especially the mural depicting dust bowl victims or Russian workers of the world uniting.

"Thomas Hart Benton," Stephen said. "Or Diego Rivera. Maybe."

"You took Art Appreciation in college?"

"Giants of Indonesian Science Fiction was full."

The floor was gray marble. From it rose columns that seemed to belong on the set of a high school production of *A Funny Thing Happened on the Way to the Forum.*

A tour was gathering. "Let's join it," I said.

"Thought we were looking for *Today.*"

"How else can we get in?"

The tour guide was a young man, blond, in a blue suit. A badge hung from the lanyard around his neck.

"He's a page," Stephen said. "Looks like a former child actor whose name I can't remember."

"Surely you jest. Thought you were a walking imdb."

"Remember those milk cartons with missing kids aged by computers? This guy's a perfect match for somebody."

We followed the crowd down the hall toward the TOUR BEGINS HERE sign.

"Oh, my God," whispered a star-struck wife to her bored-looking husband. "I can't believe we're actually here."

"*I* can't believe it costs twenty-four bucks," he mumbled.

Stephen checked his wallet. "Oops. Can you cover this one?"

"Hunter sure won't. Guess it's a worthy investment. But if you want a *Today* pom beanie or a pair of waffle slippers, you can pay for it yourself."

The wife gasped. "They have *waffle slippers*?"

"I haven't the faintest idea. Don't get your hopes up."

"I've abandoned mine," the husband muttered.

* * *

We walked between red velvet ropes, surrounded by tourists capturing everything with their smartphones.

There was a hush as we filed into an amphitheater. Seating was stadium style. Big, soft, tan chairs. The head-rests were colored like NBC's peacock—red, yellow, blue.

Sinking back, I felt like dozing. But I couldn't. What

would I do if, by some miracle, I bumped into somebody who could put me on the air?

The house lights went down; the jumbo screen came to life.

"Hi," said a familiar voice. It was *Today*'s weatherman, Al Roker. "Welcome to the National Broadcasting Network." Huge smile, but he'd lost too much weight.

Black-and-white images of old xylophones played the network's three signature tones. Then the screen went dark.

The rabble around me grew restless. "Is that *it?*" somebody asked.

Hopping onto the platform, the page held up his hand. "Sorry, folks. Technical difficulties. I know Al would want me to ask you to move in an orderly fashion from your seats to the upper level."

Stephen groaned. "But these recliners are so great. For twenty-four bucks, you'd think they could—"

"Move it," I said.

The mezzanine reminded me of the mural. "These Art Deco fixtures look like something unemployed guys cobbled together for the WPA."

"WiFi Protected Access?" Stephen asked.

"Works Progress Administration. During the Depression—"

"Okay. It's old. That's all I need to know."

I could see two oversized doors down the hall.

"The *Tonight Show*'s produced in 6B," Stephen said. "Kind of the opposite of what you're looking for."

The tour guide waved. "Studio 8H is being renovated. It was once radio's largest sound stage—now home of *Saturday Night Live*."

Stephen craned his neck and searched for a stray cast member or two, but apparently couldn't find any.

We ascended to the seventh floor Production Control rooms. Four obnoxious teenagers, most likely from the previous tour, grinned through the windows at the stage, pushing buttons and shoving levers up and down.

The page didn't seem to notice. Leading us down the steps, he held his hands aloft as if parting the Red Sea. "Please take your seats. Our tour concludes with what we like to call 'On-Air at NBC studios'. You'll all get to play a role in the production of a late-night talk show."

The set was generic—keyboard, electric guitars, drum kit, and music stands on the right, desk in the middle, sofa on the left. A fake city skyline took up the rear.

"Who'd like to be in the band?" the page asked.

Several hands shot up. Not waiting to be chosen, Stephen slipped into the aisle and ran to the stage. Others soon joined him. They began strumming and drumming and playing, quickly demonstrating their lack of musical talent. Fortunately, their instruments weren't turned on.

"We'll need a host, two guests, and a comedian," the tour guide called. A lanky, fortyish guy in Bermuda shorts and Letterman jersey loped to the desk and sat behind it. The waffle-slider wife, husband in hand, took her place on the couch and glared until he surrendered.

That was pretty much the whole group. Figured I'd be the audience, but no such luck.

The page pointed at me. "Ma'am, *you* look funny."

"Thanks a bunch."

"Come on up. We've got jokes. All you have to do is deliver them."

Reminding myself this was my only route to discrediting Rosenthal, I trudged to a large, duct-tape X on the platform

"Can you see the teleprompter?"

"I'm afraid so."

"I'll give you your cue."

Suddenly a generic theme song I'd never heard blared from a speaker. The would-be musicians went into action like a class of preschoolers with blocks, kazoos, and triangles.

"From New York," began an unseen announcer, "it's *Just Before Midnight!* And here's your host, Templeton Greeley!"

Recorded applause exploded.

The Letterman clone leaned forward and squinted at the prompter. "Our first guest is a young performer who's killing it in comedy clubs from Altoona to Mission Beach. Please welcome . . . Pat Farnsworth!"

Frozen on my mark, I started to read. The lines scrolled so fast I could barely keep up.

"Knock, knock. Who's there? Orange. Orange you mad you had to pay twenty-four bucks to see me?"

Canned applause.

"Why did the confused individual throw his or her clock out the window? He or she wanted to see time fly."

More canned applause. My armpits were soaked. I'd heard of flop sweat, but this was more like Niagara Falls.

Taking a deep breath, I wished the prompter would break down. It didn't.

"And in conclusion, here's the best joke I ever heard. Bought some shoes from a drug dealer. Don't know what he *laced* them with, but I was *tripping* all day!"

Still more artificial applause. The recorded band went into overdrive. With a prayer of confession, I stumbled off the stage.

The host proceeded to interview the lucky couple. By the time they were through, divorce seemed inevitable.

The volunteer orchestra faked a tinny finale. The tour guide congratulated us. "If you'd like to see what you just created, go to nbc.com/midnight/dat451xcf3 for your digital download."

Stephen took out his phone and went on the prowl.

The page passed out peacock pins. "Included in the ticket price! Come back and see us sometime."

We followed him to The Shop at NBC Studios. Stephen showed me his phone. "Wait 'til you see this. You'd better hope nobody else does."

When we got to the gift shop, he wanted to borrow $275 to buy a coffee mug autographed by the late Ed McMahon.

I shook my head. "Have a short-term memory problem? You're on the hook for your own souvenirs."

He grudgingly settled for a $5 mechanical pencil that said OUR PRIDE IS SHOWING.

"Hurry up and pay," I said. "Then let's find the *Today* office before the place closes."

* * *

I asked the girl at the register where the *Today* show offices were.

"Studio's on the ground floor. Offices off-limits to visitors without an appointment."

"Sounds promising."

We located the studio and the famous windows where sign-bearing fans proclaimed their love for the hosts, jumping up and down like antifa on helium.

None of them were around at the moment, but two women stepped from behind a curtain and grabbed their purses from a desk.

"Hoda Kotb and Savannah Guthrie," Stephen whispered.

They started to leave, but I wended my way around the cameras and sound equipment.

"Excuse me," I called. "One of your producers contacted me a few days ago about appearing as a guest, and I turned him down. It was about the prison riot. I've changed my mind. If you're still interested, I'll do it."

"Oh, yeah," said Hoda. "I remember you."

Savannah checked her watch. "We're on our way out, but I'll find somebody you can talk to. Just a minute."

She disappeared behind the curtain, then returned with a young woman pulling off a pair of headphones.

"This is Amber. Good luck."

She and Hoda left.

The girl looked suspicious. "What's this all about?"

"We have some information we think your viewers would be interested in."

"*Really* interested," Stephen said.

She motioned for us to sit down.

"Five minutes to convince me."

CHAPTER 20

I BEGAN TO DESCRIBE WHAT HAPPENED IN THE RIOT. Stephen kept chiming in with descriptive details about smoke and noise, adding nothing but subtracting from my time.

"Then I got this call from your producer. Think his name was Peter."

Amber nodded. "Peter O'Dell."

"I'm going as fast as I can, no thanks to certain people who can't shut up."

"Good, because things move quickly in the news business. We've almost lost our window. The riot's ancient history—or will be by the end of the week."

Taking her phone from her pocket, she pressed her thumb to the screen. "Here's the schedule. We could fit you in day after tomorrow. Rachael Ray cancelled. Too bad. She was going to show how to make really expensive dog food. I've got a little Pomeranian who eats enough to—"

"Moving right along," Stephen interrupted. "Riots are

great, but here's the main event. We've dug up some dynamite stuff about two crooked import houses right here in New York. You won't believe what they've done."

"I'm confused," she said. "Import houses? We can only deal with one story at a time. Sounds like a job for the News Department."

Stephen wilted. Disappointed. So was I.

She wrote a number on a slip of paper. "Got a friend over there. Assignment editor."

"Thanks," I said.

"Anything else?"

"About clothes—"

"Wear something simple. No weird patterns, nothing flashy. You're not allowed to outshine Hoda or Savannah."

"What should *I* wear?" Stephen asked.

"Anything you want. We don't have a dress code for the audience."

"But I was in the riot, too."

"Hiding under the table," I muttered.

Narrowing his eyes, he took his NBC pen from his pocket and held it up. "*Your* pride is showing."

* * *

Back home in Connecticut the next morning, I tried to call the assignment editor. Couldn't reach him.

I opened my closet and walked in. Nothing weird except the pirate outfit I'd worn three years ago to the Halloween office party where Hunter forced everyone to bob for cantaloupe. He thought it would float.

Nothing worth wearing, either. Not on national TV. Or even local.

After breakfast I drove to Ross Dress for Less. Found just the thing on the clearance rack—a dark blue business suit with a cigarette burn on the lower back. Couldn't figure out how anybody could get a hole like that in a place like that, but it would be perfect as long as I didn't turn around.

In the parking lot I called Mikki.

"Just bought a new outfit at Ross. You should come down here sometime. Check out the seconds."

"Maybe next week. Why'd you need new clothes?"

"Going to be on *Today*. Tomorrow."

"So which is it?"

"The *Today* show. Tomorrow. To talk about the riot. And hopefully imports."

"Oh, wish I could be in the audience. But I've gotta work. There's a little TV in the break room. Maybe I can catch you there."

"Good. I need you to tell me how I did."

"What'll you say about the big fight between Icarus and Rosenthal?"

"Don't know yet. The *Today* people don't want me to talk about that. But I can't get hold of the News Department."

"What's your outfit like?"

I described it.

"*Cigarette burn?* What are you, homeless? Got a great dress I can loan you. Bright red with a gold scarf."

"Thanks, but I don't want to look like Joan Collins. And I'm not a size six like you. Heard the saying about fifty pounds of flour in a five-pound sack?"

"Yeah, but you sure it was flour?"

"I was cleaning it up."

"Have to go. I smell the boss."

I got off the line and tried the assignment editor again. This time I got his assistant.

"He's in Italy on vacation. Can't take any story suggestions until he's back. Sorry."

She hung up.

I knew what I had to do.

It was already giving me a headache.

* * *

You sure have to get up early for *Today*. I'd gotten two hours of sleep, worrying about how it would go.

At 6:00 a.m. I found myself staring at a makeup mirror near the studio, trying to blink the crust out of my eyes.

A more energetic woman, evidently fueled by the coffee in her peacock mug, was applying enough foundation to my face to cover a multitude of sins. An eyebrow pencil was clamped between her teeth.

I tapped my foot nervously on the ring of the stool I sat on. "How long have you been doing this?"

"Too long," she answered, clearly loath to go into detail.

Amber walked in, headphones still around her neck. "Hoda was going to interview you this morning, but she's got the flu. We've got a guest host."

"Who?"

"Mitt Powers."

"Who's that?"

She laughed. "Just the guy who won an Emmy for getting the last interview with Fidel Castro. Made the old man cry. Does the same thing with lying politicians and sweaty tycoons."

I found enough energy to groan.

"Don't move your head," the makeup woman said. "If I stab you with the eyebrow pencil, they make me buy a new one."

"Not to worry," Amber said, patting me on the shoulder. "He's mellowed out since he married a woman half his age. Or maybe he's just tired."

She consulted her watch. "You're on in seven minutes."

When she was gone, the cosmetologist snickered. "Ain't life grand?"

* * *

I tried calling Mikki for moral support but got no answer.

A few minutes later, a page hustled in and ushered me to a chair on the set. The lights nearly blinded me. I was pretty sure Stephen was out there somewhere.

I set my purse on the floor. The import documents were inside. I gulped half the bottle of water from the table near my chair. Hoped I wouldn't have to go to the bathroom.

A tall man in a dark gray suit and light gray hair stepped onto the set. "I'm Mitt Powers." His smile looked programmed.

"So you got stuck in the middle of that conflagration," he added. "The prison thing. My wife tells me you're a new icon of female empowerment."

"Not at the moment," I said, my voice cracking.

He settled into the other chair. A technician clipped on our microphones.

"Three cameras," Powers said. "Don't look directly

into them. Stick with me or the audience. The one with the red light is on."

"Sixty seconds," a voice called from the darkness.

"That's the floor director," Powers added. A man stepped into the light, counted down with his fingers, then pointed at the host.

The theme played, then faded as he welcomed viewers.

I told myself it would all be over soon—the interview, my jackhammer pulse. Maybe my career.

He turned to me. "Carolyn Neville recently found herself in the midst of a prison riot. She was drafted to negotiate with the leaders. Some say her courage makes her another Gloria Steinem."

He read a description of what happened from the teleprompter, then paused. I guessed I was supposed to answer.

"I did what anybody would do. It's no fun to look down the barrel of an automatic rifle, but I had a good friend who was doing it in a cell. At least I had a hole in the wall to climb through."

There were some *ooohs* from the audience, but mostly laughs.

The floor director put his fists forward and mimed snapping a celery stick in half.

"We'll be back after this message," Powers said.

Sagging against my seat, I chugged the rest of the water.

Amber approached Powers and told him about the next guest.

After the break he turned to me. "Carolyn Neville, anything you'd care to add about your narrow escape from these domestic terrorists?"

I felt dizzy. My bladder started issuing storm warnings.

I took the papers from my purse. "A few things about a crime that's almost as serious. A scandal involving a major import company. Happens to be based here in New York."

This time it was Powers who looked confused.

At the edge of the set Amber glared at me and made a throat-cutting gesture.

I pressed on, trying not to sound like a complete idiot. At any moment security guards might carry me off.

"This has to do with fraud, endangering children, and using arson against a competitor."

Powers raised a hand. "Now let me get this straight. You're saying this about one of the most successful companies in America?"

I nodded.

"Too bad we're out of time. That's a pretty potent accusation. We're not going to jump to any conclusions, and everyone involved will need a chance to clear the air. I'm sure our News Department will want to talk with you further."

"But they're not—"

He conjured up the fake smile again and faced the camera. "When we come back, a computer so small it'll fit under your fingernail. But why would you want that? You'll be surprised."

The director broke another celery stick.

"*You* won't be back," Powers said. "I can guarantee *that.*"

Amber returned and stood there, waiting for me to get up. The technician unclipped my microphone.

"Hope you can find your way out." It sounded like *Goodbye forever.*

I nodded, then stumbled into darkness.

Heading for the rear of the studio, I ran into Stephen.

"Wow," he said.

"At least he didn't make me cry."

"Huh?"

Passing under the green EXIT sign, I started my search for the bathroom.

CHAPTER 21

WHILE STEPHEN AND I WAITED FOR THE ASSIGNMENT editor to return, we hid out at Pendleton House.

The first thing I did was print a photo of Joey I found on Google Images. Taking it to the security guard with the big orange glasses at the front desk, I introduced myself.

"Carolyn Neville. Book Publishing."

He put down his phone. "Yeah, I seen you plenty of times. You're usually with that scruffy kid."

"Stephen Ames."

"Lee Kirby."

I held up the picture. "This is Joey Rosenthal."

Leaning forward, he lifted his glasses from the bridge of his nose. "Uh-huh."

"Very bad guy. After Stephen and me."

"You don't say."

"Could you keep an eye out for him?"

"Sure, no problem."

I handed him my card. "Give me a call if you see him, okay?"

He patted the gun on his belt.

"I can do better than that." He winked.

"Uh . . . that won't be necessary. Just let me know if he's in the building."

He shrugged. "Have it your way."

Picking up his phone, he went back to playing something.

"Bubble Dragons," he said. "Got top score this month. Four hundred thousand. My handle's Mr. Fantastic."

"I can see why."

Back upstairs, I went into Stephen's cubicle. He was actually working, doing Track Changes on his laptop.

"I hate authors who delete all my brilliant fixes," he said. "Love to eradicate this one in particular. Thinks she knows more about *Black Mirror* than I do."

"Is that a musical group?"

"More like a perverse *Twilight Zone.* Why are you holding a picture of Joey?"

"Got the security guard keeping an eye out for him."

"The one with the orange glasses?"

"He offered to kill the man for us."

"A little extreme. Let's take a raincheck."

Hearing throat-clearing behind me, I turned. It was Hunter. His face was impassive, like one of those robots on *Westworld.*

"Missed the *Today* show. But a member of the board told me about your appearance."

He waited for me to gasp, faint, or sink to my knees and beg for mercy. But I was wearing a skirt.

I could almost hear facial motors tighten his lips into a cruel frown. "You're going to get us sued one way or the other."

"We're trying to solve the Joey problem."

"By humiliating him on national TV?"

"No, by showing he's a victimizer, not a victim. Nobody's going to feel sorry for a guy whose family chokes children and burns down buildings."

For a moment his eyes seemed to light up like hot coals, but I think it was my imagination. "No one will feel sorry for you when you're fired for exposing us to this kind of risk."

"We're trying to meet with NBC's assignment editor. If we can interest him in the story, presto—problem solved."

"Not by a long shot."

"Well, almost. But we have proof of the company's pattern of behavior."

"More or less," Stephen said.

Hunter's head swiveled, then stopped. I could swear I heard a *click*.

"Time's almost up. If I were you, I'd update my resumé."

His left eye twitched, then fluttered.

Or perhaps I imagined that, too.

* * *

Next day we finally met with the assignment editor, Wallace Holt, in his office.

He was surprisingly young, wiry, with thick black hair and big eyes to match. His office was a mess.

He shrugged. "There's a guy at Fox Business Network who says anyone with a neat desk's not a reporter."

After we sat down, he pushed two glass bowls of candy toward us. "Just got back from vacation. Got these in Venice. This one's *Gommose Morbide alla Liquirizia.*"

Stephen made a face. "Looks like licorice to me."

"If you're thinking of American licorice, this is better. Soft."

"Not a licorice man."

"Me neither," I said.

"That one's *Caramelle Scaramellini Spicchi Su,*" he explained. "Fruit-flavored. Take your pick."

Our fingers both went for the latter. I pulled back long enough for Stephen to grab a handful. Picking out a single piece, he unwrapped it.

"I watched the tape of your interview," Wallace said. "Went pretty well 'til you sent it off track."

"Mr. Powers made *that* abundantly clear. But this is an important story. I just wanted to—"

"That's not how this works. You don't bait-and-switch, then hold the host hostage while you deliver your manifesto. After your experience at the prison, I'd think you'd understand that."

Taking one of the licorice candies, he flicked it into the air with his thumb and caught it in his mouth. Then he stared at me with those eyes, waiting.

"Okay, you're right," I said. "Shoot the messenger if you want, but it's still a message worth hearing." I popped the confection in my mouth. It melted almost immediately.

"Good, huh?" Stephen asked. "I'm on my fourth."

Wallace slid his laptop in front of him. "Give me the high points."

I went over the clash of the import titans and showed him the documents.

He rubbed the spot between his eyes. "I can't go with this. Our legal people would have a fit. And it's not like it's a national story."

"Icarus and Rosenthal provide about fifty-six percent of low-cost imported toys, tools, and soft goods to

American stores. They're on the stock exchanges. And don't your viewers like to hear about crooked rich guys?"

He set the papers on his desk. "Can I make copies?"

I nodded.

"I'll have somebody look into it. No promises."

He picked up the phone. A young woman with glasses almost as big as the guard's came in. "This is our intern, Kathy."

Nodding shyly, she took the papers and left.

Stephen scooped up another handful of candies, unwrapped three, and tried the tossing and catching trick. Bouncing off his face, they landed on the carpet.

Wallace stared at him. "What's *your* role in all this? Candy tester? Village idiot?"

Stephen bent down and retrieved the errant sweets. "Just a humble representative of the eighteen to forty-nine demographic."

"Can't imagine how you got elected."

Kathy returned and handed over the papers.

Wallace waved goodbye to us. "Your cue to exit."

Stephen put the candies in his mouth. "A little fuzzy, but good."

"Gross," Wallace said.

* * *

We spent the next 24 hours or so putting out fires and wrestling errant authors. Stephen Tracked so many Changes he made me promise to poison that writer next time I took her to lunch.

About 11:00 a.m. I got a call from the security guard. "It's that guy you told me about. What you want me to do?"

"Tell him I'm not here."

There was silence. Then Kirby was back. "He's gone."

I swallowed. "Did he leave or get in an elevator?"

"Don't know. He's not in the lobby."

"*That's* not good."

"Sorry. You gonna be okay?"

"Ask me in about fifteen minutes."

CHAPTER 22

"THINK WE SHOULD TAKE THE ELEVATOR TO THE FIRST floor and drive away?" Stephen asked.

I checked my watch. "No, let's hide in Hunter's office."

"Just like that, you get to decide?"

"Who signs your paycheck?"

"Some guy in Finance. His penmanship sucks."

"And who decides whether you get paid in the first place?"

"You."

"To Hunter's office, then."

Our boss was on the phone when we entered his man cave. Whoever was on the other end couldn't get a word in edgewise.

"And another thing," the Anointed One continued. "Next time you drop my football trophy in the toilet, don't try to flush it."

He slammed the phone down and pushed himself back from the desk. "What do you two want?"

"Just heard from the security guard. Joey Rosenthal may have gotten past him."

They always talk about people turning pale, but it never happens fast enough to see. Hunter's complexion didn't lighten, but he seemed to lose at least two pints of hemoglobin in about twelve seconds.

"Police," he whispered. Picking up the phone, he dialed.

"Hold on," I said. "They can't send enough officers to search the building. There isn't time."

He put the receiver back in its cradle. "If we get out of this alive, I'll fire you. If not, I'll leave a note in your personnel files recommending posthumous retroactive discharge."

Stephen leaned toward me. "Sounds messy."

With a *bang* the door burst open. Hunter leapt to his feet.

It was Joey, leading the panicky admin by the arm.

She was panting. "I tried to stop him. But . . . I've never had much upper body strength. Especially when the other body has a gun."

* * *

Despite the sidearm poking the poor woman in the back, Joey looked happier than a grave digger with a new backhoe.

"Tried your office first, Carolyn. But that was too obvious. Not to mention empty."

He tucked the gun in his belt and shoved the admin into Hunter's arms. She wriggled away, wrecking her chances of filing a sexual harassment suit.

"Let's play a little game," Joey said. "I'll be the judge. You're the jury. Except you don't get a vote."

He turned to Stephen and me. "You're the defendants. Thicke, you're an accomplice. I'll deal with you later."

"Pardon my impertinence," I said. "The first place to handle this is in court."

"And the *last* place to do it is on TV with half the freakin' country watching. Lawyer tells me he could sue your butts for defamation. Only I'm not that patient. My ex-wife noticed that about me, too."

Hunter stepped back from his admin, who looked like she was trying to wake herself from a bad dream.

Going to the window, he gazed at a bank of storm clouds. "I know where you're coming from, Mr. Rosenthal. When I was nine, I was the skinny kid who got picked last for dodge ball. Even my teammates threw the ball at me." He paused for effect. "Sometimes life stings."

Joey grabbed a tissue from a box on the desk and wiped away an imaginary tear. "Oh, I give up," he said with a fake sob. "You go sit in the corner. You don't get to play."

Hunter sat in the corner next to his putter and a potted plant. I could see his Adam's apple bob.

After settling into the upper management chair, our opponent set the gun in his lap. "Round one."

He smiled. "Ms. Neville, is it true that you accused my company of killing kids and burning down buildings on the *Today* show? I wasn't watching, but my lawyer got a copy."

I nodded.

"Can you prove that stuff?"

"I think so."

"Not if you're dead."

"That would be an impediment."

He turned to Stephen. "Who are you again?"

"Innocent bystander."

"Talk about *lame*. I met you at the garage, remember? I bet you stink as a musician. That's reason enough to take you out. World's full of drummers who don't know the difference between a snare and a bongo."

"I'm a guitarist."

"That's even worse. How many fingers does it take to make a B-flat chord?"

"Four."

He snorted. "Don't have to be Les Paul to know *that*."

"Can we get to round two?" I asked.

He shook his head. "Game over. I got a rehearsal to get back to."

Rising from the chair, he looked around the room.

"If you shoot us, the police will know exactly who did it," I said.

"Maybe. But I'm not gonna wait around to find out. Got just enough money left in my trust to find a nice place in Mexico. Won't need to fire a single shot."

He turned to Hunter. "What floor we on?"

"Third." The Anointed One sounded like a dog's squeaky toy.

"That should do it. How you open one of these windows?"

"With a battering ram," I said. "It's a skyscraper, not a grade school."

Hunter piped up. "Smaller one on the right has a crank. Only used it a few times when the air conditioning was broken."

I covered my eyes with my hands. "Thanks. With friends like you—"

Joey sighed. "Gonna be a terrible accident. Guess they won't rule it a mass suicide, but you never know. Either way, I'm outta here. Line up in order of height. No, scratch that. Ladies first."

The admin collapsed in a chair. I put my hand on her shoulder.

Rosenthal pointed at Hunter. "Open the window."

He got up and tried to turn the crank. Didn't move.

"Help him out," Joey told Stephen.

Working together, they finally got it open.

I could hear the wind whistle.

***

"Which of you girls wants to go first?" Joey asked.

I tried to imagine standing at the pearly gates and explaining why I stuck a lit firecracker in Charlie Simmons' underwear in fourth grade. Wasn't the first time I'd sent off a desperate prayer in the last 20 years, but it might be the last.

Stepping toward the window, I felt the wind on my face. Cool, but not comforting.

"Come on now," Joey said. "From what I've read, this doesn't take but a few seconds."

I heard the admin whimper behind me. My heart was hammering.

"Changed my mind," he said.

I put my hand against the glass, feeling faint. "I thought you—"

He snickered. "What do you think I am, crazy? Four murder charges? That's the last thing I need."

Reaching around me, he cranked the window shut. "I believe we can come to an understanding."

"What do you want?" Hunter asked, his face drained of another pint.

"Think of this as a demonstration. You push me too far, and who knows—I just might do something irrational. You've got some papers that make me look bad.

Give them to me and we'll call it square. Stay away from reporters and this whole thing'll blow over. Won't sue for defamation. Got better ways to spend my money."

I put my hands on my hips. "What's the catch?"

"Isn't any. Go ahead and publish your stupid book. We'll just put this behind us."

"How do we know we can trust you?" Stephen asked.

"You don't. But you can be sure that if I send you out a third-story window, you'll be flat *and* broke."

He chucked me under the chin, which I hated, and patted Hunter's cheek. The admin staggered to the potted plant and looked like she was about to do something unpleasant.

Joey picked up the putter and tossed it to me. "Remember those papers. If you don't, you may need this for protection."

He shut the door behind him.

I handed the club to Hunter. "Couldn't have done it without you."

CHAPTER 23

We all stood there, stunned.

The admin took a deep breath and backed away from the potted plant.

Hunter tapped me on the shoulder with his putter. "I could call the police."

I shook my head. "We can't prove he threatened us with a gun. Besides, this is our chance to put the whole suit behind us."

"Have to get those papers to him," Stephen said. "He doesn't know Wallace Holt has copies. What do we do about that?"

"Nothing. Even if Holt follows through, Joey's right. It'll blow over. He's got a great lawyer."

I paused. "I'll send them via courier. Mikki can return the Icarus originals to her boss."

The three of us went down to lunch in the Pendleton cafeteria. The admin didn't feel like eating.

I got greens, even though they'd stopped putting real bleu cheese on the salad bar. Hunter had a hamburger and banana. Stephen chose nachos, chocolate milk, and two of those plastic-looking Drumstick ice cream cones.

Hunter stole ketchup and mustard from a nearby table. "Our Friends in Legal will knight us for avoiding the lawsuit. When the book's a bestseller, the board will double my stock options."

I shook pepper on my salad. "I doubt that."

"What? That they'll knight us? Or that I'll get more stock?"

"Both. I don't think Kathleen's going to make the list, either."

"You're such an elitist."

"You mean *defeatist?*"

"I believe it can be spelled either way." He shook the mustard over his burger. The cap came off, dumping a blob of yellow the size of a sunflower on the bun. Swearing, he reached for a napkin.

"Karma," Stephen whispered to me.

"I just want to get back to solving Roger's murder," I said. "That should make Legal even happier. Especially Gina."

After his fourth napkin, Hunter gave up. "You two have work to do. And I don't mean playing Columbo."

"We'll get it done." I turned to Stephen, who was dipping one of his cones in the chocolate milk. "I hereby dub thee Interim Executive Senior Editor for the duration."

"I want a raise."

I took a five-dollar bill from my purse and handed it to him.

"There's more where that came from. But not for you."

* * *

After lunch I struck out on my own.

Hunter's admin being indisposed, I sent the papers to Joey by courier. I stopped by Icarus Imports and handed the originals to Mikki.

"We had a visit from Joey. Threatened us with a gun. Acted like he was going to throw us out the window."

"What the—"

"He didn't actually do it."

She put the papers in her desk drawer. "I'm through with this industrial espionage stuff. My job sucks, but I need to keep it."

"Consider yourself retired. No more Inspector Gadget, I promise."

Back in the car, I called Detective Spiner. When I told her what happened with Rosenthal, there was a long silence.

"Want to press charges?"

"Can't prove anything."

"Yeah. Saves me having to fill out a lot of forms."

"Do you have any leads on the murder?"

"One of the suspects has flown the coop. The Major. Makes my job a little easier. Too many suspects anyway."

"What do you mean, 'flown the coop'?"

"Disappeared. We'll look for him, but missing persons who aren't kids or mental patients aren't high priority. Besides, he can't get far on one leg."

I resisted the urge to lecture her about ableism. "Maybe he disappeared because he's guilty."

"Only makes him look guiltier. Where's he going to go?"

"If you find him, let me know."

"Right."

Hanging up, I tried to think of somewhere he might hide. There was something in his unpublished manuscript about a safehouse in Trenton where agents and witnesses could stay. The brass went crazy when they read that one.

He wasn't an agent anymore, but might still have contacts who could get him in temporarily. Not everybody in the intelligence community thought he was a traitor.

Back at the office I found my file on his book. He'd listed a source, a fellow cyberwarrior named Anthony Dean. He lived in New Mexico or had a few years ago.

Calling, I got voicemail. Strange that his message didn't mention his name. Or maybe not.

Finally he picked up. "Yes?"

I explained who I was, and that his friend might be in danger.

"Is this a secure line?"

"Um . . . don't know."

"Is it your cell?"

"No, a landline."

He sighed. "Guess I can chance it. But make it quick."

"The safehouse. Where is it?"

He hesitated. "I think Buck got a raw deal from the feds. But how can I tell you—"

"He's missing, and I just want to make sure he's okay."

Another pause. Finally, he gave the address. "Thirty-four Livingston Avenue."

"Thanks."

"You've got to keep my name out of this. The CIA and NSA have long memories."

The line went dead.

* * *

That night I drove to the address, parked, and waited.

The place looked like a typical middle-class residence built around 1950, tan clapboard siding. Oak trees towered in the front yard. A tire swing hung from the biggest.

I knocked on the door.

An elderly woman answered. With both hands she gripped a walker.

"I'm looking for Major Buck Dijon," I said.

"Sorry, Dear. I've never heard of him."

I looked over her shoulder. Two men in white shirts and ties sat at a table in the living room. One played solitaire. The other muttered into a walkie-talkie.

Clearly I'd come to the right place, but for all I knew the old lady had a revolver in the walker's basket.

"My mistake," I said.

With a nod she shut the door.

Retreating to the sidewalk, I spotted something shiny in the bushes. Stepping toward it, I saw a cell phone on the ground. Then a black Oxford shoe.

I parted the foliage.

The Major lay there and wasn't breathing.

CHAPTER 24

DIALING 911, I TRIED TO REMEMBER THE CPR COURSE I'D taken when I was a Girl Scout. The dispatcher said an ambulance was on the way.

The Major was already on his back. I opened his mouth, felt around with my finger. Guessed his airway was open.

Was it ten chest compressions and three rescue breaths? Or ten rescue breaths and twenty compressions? I decided to split the difference. Fifteen blows to his thorax and half a dozen puffs of air.

I'd never actually done this before. Oh, I'd kissed at least four guys, but never had the urge to match lips with one this cold.

His breath smelled like Juicy Fruit gum. He needed a shave.

The front door opened and one of the shirt-sleeved guys came out. "What the heck are you doing?"

Jumping down from the porch, he got his answer. Swearing, he got down on one knee.

"Told him not to go outside."

I had plenty of questions but was too busy mashing the Major's breastbone and hyperventilating to ask.

Mr. Shirtsleeves was about to take over when I heard a siren. An ambulance pulled up, followed by a squad car. Two paramedics got out and went to work.

The mysterious agent, or whatever he was, helped me up and led me back to the porch.

"You're a regular Florence Nightingale. But you've got some explaining to do."

Still shaking, I sat down on the railing. I gave him my name and tried to justify my presence.

"You're in over your head," he said. "Dean never should have told you about this place. But you haven't actually done anything illegal. Tell anybody about this, though, and you'll be in so much trouble you'll have to find your *own* place to hide."

He loosened his tie and went back in the house.

I stared at the ambulance. I could still taste the gum.

After about five minutes, the paramedics give up. One pulled a body bag from the vehicle and zipped the Major inside. I turned away.

One of the two officers from the squad car came over. "Ma'am, did you discover the body?"

I nodded.

"I know this is a bad time, but we have a few questions."

"If it's all the same to you, I'd like to talk with Detective Spiner."

"You know her?"

"Yeah." I took out my phone. She was on speed dial now.

When she picked up, I gave her the short version.

"Don't go anywhere," she replied. "I'll be there in ten minutes."

* * *

A woman from the coroner's office showed up and briefly examined the corpse. She filled out some forms, then left.

The paramedics took the body away. I wondered whether Buck had any family. I wondered what would become of his poems.

Spiner pulled up with a young male technician who started taking pictures and looking for evidence.

I gave the detective the rest of the story, leaving out the part about this being a safehouse. Someone had to be listening.

She took down the details and shook her head. "Man, this is above my pay grade. Last thing I need is to get tangled up with a bunch of spies, or whatever they are. But it's a homicide, and we've got jurisdiction unless they say otherwise."

"Can I go yet?"

"Hang on. Did you see any wounds, blood, or signs of strangulation?"

"No. But maybe the coroner's office did. One of their people just left."

She turned to the technician. "Anything yet?"

He scratched his chin. "Probably killed nearby, then dragged into the bushes. No bullet casing, no weapon. Could have been poisoned. Won't know for a couple of days at least."

"He had an artificial leg, you know," I said.

She put her pad in her pocket. "Not sure what that has to do with anything. You can go, but don't be surprised if you have to tell this story 'til you're sick of it."

"Already am."

She returned to her car.

Brushing the leaves and dirt from my knees, I took one more look at the house. Through the window I saw the old lady's silhouette. No doubt she was watching me.

* * *

I drove home, exhausted, and called Stephen. When I told him what happened, he whistled.

"Jeez. Must mean Dijon couldn't be the murderer."

"Depends on who killed him. Must have thought somebody was after him. Otherwise, why go to the safehouse?"

"Which of the suspects was most likely to kill somebody this way?"

"Hard to say, since we don't know how he died. The police think he may have been killed somewhere else."

"Guess we can rule out suicide."

"Not funny."

"What do you want to do next?"

"Sleep."

I watched the news, which ignored *my* top story, then crawled into bed.

For half an hour I stared at the ceiling, then got up and brewed two cups of Sleep Tea with melatonin.

After bracing two chairs against the door, I went back to bed.

CHAPTER 25

In the morning, I realized my paranoia. I was nobody's target at the moment.

But I felt obligated to attend Major Dijon's funeral.

After making a cup of coffee I found my last donut in the breadbox. Then checked the newspaper, thinking his murder might be covered. It wasn't.

I called Anthony Dean.

He swore. "So they finally got him."

"I'm planning to go the memorial service."

"It'll be a military one, even with all the controversy about the book. Buck was honorably discharged. I'll look into it for you. Not sure if I'll go myself."

I finished my donut. There was a knock at the door. I was still in my bathrobe.

Squinting through the peephole I saw two ramrod-straight Air Force officers, looking impatient. One checked his watch.

I opened the door.

The taller one took off his hat. "Carolyn Neville?"

"Yes."

"Lieutenant Hopkins. This is Corporal Adkins. May we come in?"

Pulling my robe tighter, I let them in and turned off the stove.

They continued to stand.

"You discovered the body of Major Bernard Dijon?" asked the lieutenant.

"I thought his name was Buck."

"A nickname," said the corporal. "What was your involvement with him?"

"I knew him through work. We were going to publish his book, but there were legal problems. And he shared some of his poems with me."

The officers looked at each other. "Were you aware he was an agent?" the lieutenant asked.

"As in *spy?*"

"We believe he was pressured to divulge sensitive information to a certain foreign government. Things he didn't put in the book."

I just stared.

The lieutenant folded his arms. "In your association with him, did you ever hear him allude to Project North Star? Or the letters *E-M-C-O-D?*"

"Not that I remember."

He relaxed, but only slightly.

"Sorry to bother you. We'd appreciate it if you didn't mention this conversation to anyone."

"All right." I stood up. "Do you know when his funeral will be?"

"I believe it's Friday. The family's been notified. I'm sure it'll be in the paper."

He put his hat back on.

Pivoting smartly toward the door, they let themselves out.

* * *

On Friday, we attended the Major's funeral at Cypress Hills National Cemetery. It looked like Arlington, but smaller, white tombstones arranged crisscross fashion, fenced in by wrought iron.

Stephen and I, both dressed in the blackest outfits we could find, stepped out of the car.

"Must be ninety degrees," he said. "The wind doesn't help."

A hearse was parked by a gazebo the size of a bandstand where John Philip Sousa might wave his baton. No more than a dozen people fanning themselves with programs sat on the brown benches.

The white casket was on its way, carried by six men. Half were soldiers, half civilian.

A three-man honor guard, two men and a woman, stood by in blue uniforms and sunglasses. They snapped their white-gloved hands in salute.

The pallbearers placed the casket on a coffin cart.

Two other soldiers, expressionless, unrolled a flag and held it lengthwise between them like a sheet. After folding it in triangles, they presented it to an elderly woman in the first row. Her head was bowed. She nodded.

"His mother," I whispered. "Has to be. Strange. I never thought of him as having one."

A chaplain took the podium. It looked like the pulpit at my church, before our pastor took to roaming the platform with a little microphone and earplug.

The eulogy was short. I wondered whether the speaker had ever met Buck. The latter had never struck me as the religious type.

After citing the usual obituary factoids, the chaplain

took a paper out of his pocket. "I'm told the Major was a poet. His mother would like me to share an example of his work at this time. Perhaps this best sums up his view of life and will serve to comfort you today."

He cleared his throat.

Three roads diverged inside a wood.
One was best, one was worst;
The third was merely good.
A traveler in humble garb
One dismal, rainy night
By happenstance did come upon
The junction at the light.
"Now must I choose the path to take
Which leads to joy and peace;
If only a sage would come this way
My misery would cease.
The tortured soul did wait and wait
Until the dawn broke through;
But no wise guide came down the road
To tell him what to do.
And so it is within this veil
Of suffering and pain;
We each must judge what things are true
And what will grant us gain.
So like that pilgrim let us vow
To trod the trail alone;
No one will come to ease our plight;
Our destiny is bone.

"My God," Stephen whispered. Someone in the back row sobbed.

Shaking his head, the chaplain folded up the paper. "Peace be with you," he said.

The honor guard picked up its rifles and stood next to the casket. Aiming skyward, they fired three times.

A bugler stepped up and raised his instrument. The brass glistened in the sun, as did his forehead.

The plaintive sound of taps echoed. The soldiers all retreated. The guests got to their feet.

A young man with mussed blond hair and John Lennon sunglasses approached, glancing over his shoulder.

He stuck out his hand. "Anthony Dean. Recognize you from the Pendleton website."

"I thought you weren't coming."

"Changed my mind. Buck didn't have a lot of friends."

"What'd you think of that poem?" Stephen said.

"I'm not a critic. That's the first one I've heard."

I sighed. "I think he wrote one about hope, but I can't remember it."

"Well, I've got to get going," Dean said. "Don't think I can handle meeting his mom."

He walked toward the parking lot, keeping his head down.

"Come on," I told Stephen. "Somebody's got to say hello to the poor woman."

We introduced ourselves to the Major's mother. She seemed a little lost, clinging to the folded flag.

"He was all I had. I hardly ever saw him, but he called once a week. The government treated him so badly, you know."

"We do," I said. "We're doing our best to find out what happened."

"Thank you."

"Do you have someone to take you home?"

"Yes, one of the soldiers brought me. A nice lieutenant."

She sat and waited.

"God bless you," I said.

We were halfway to the car when Detective Spiner walked up.

"Missed the whole thing," she said. "Wanted to pay my respects, but also thought you'd like to know the cause of death."

"Which was?" I asked.

"Poison. Probably something he ate."

I looked around. "Seems he didn't have a lot of friends."

"Maybe not. But all he needed was one enemy."

* * *

On the way back to Pendleton House, we got caught in a traffic jam.

"Who do you suppose was on the major's enemies list?" Stephen asked.

I tapped the steering wheel. "You mean *his* enemies?"

"Either way."

"Well, half the U.S. government. And from the looks of it, some foreign ones, too."

"I think we should—"

His phone rang.

"Hello?"

He paused, listening. "Liza Boxer," he whispered, then put her on speaker.

"Stephen?"

"Right here."

"I've got something to give you." She sounded coy as a third grader with a valentine. "But I'm stuck at home with carpal tunnel syndrome."

"What is it?"

"I thought you knew. It's an injury caused by repetitive motion."

"Not that. What's the *present?*"

"It's a secret, silly."

"We're in the middle of traffic, but we'll stop off when we can."

"I read about Major Dijon in the paper. It's so sad. I can't imagine why anyone would poison him. The man was a *poet,* for goodness' sake."

"How'd you know he was poisoned? *We* just found out."

"I went to the paper's electronic version. Breaking news."

After hanging up, Stephen checked out the website. Sure enough, it was there.

"What are you looking for?" I asked.

"Just checking. I don't believe in psychics."

CHAPTER 26

WE DROVE SLOWLY IN SILENCE FOR SEVERAL MINUTES.

"You know," I said, "Buck's death may have had nothing to do with Roger. If he was some kind of agent, plenty of people could have wanted him out of the picture. And spies use poison, right?"

"In the movies. Usually bite down on a pill. Russians are always killing their own guys with plutonium, though. Ought to use borscht. Cheaper, but just as lethal."

We passed a car wreck, a Beamer crumpled under a semi. Fire truck, ambulance, three cop cars.

I kept my eyes on the road, but Stephen rubber-necked. "God, what a mess."

Traffic began to speed up.

I checked my watch. "Just about dinner time. There's a granola bar in the glove compartment."

He popped the box open and felt around. "Nothing here but the manual and some papers. Can't we stop somewhere?"

"As I recall, no gas, food, or lodging for another forty minutes or so."

He stuck his hand in again, but it came out empty. His low growl reminded me of a junkyard dog we'd met in Colorado.

"Don't think we'll ever know what really happened with Dijon," I said. "Those two guys in the safehouse looked like they could cover their tracks pretty well."

"So do we cross him off the list?"

"Let's just move him to the bottom. What we *really* need is to concentrate on Gina. We won't get squat from Spiner, but maybe her lawyer can. The police have to share that stuff with the defense, don't they? Discovery or something?"

"Guess so."

"Then let's find out tomorrow what we can discover. In the meantime—"

"Hey, we just passed a Red Robin. And a Pizza Hut."

"Next exit. I promise." My stomach gurgled.

"Was that you? Pretty unladylike."

"What is this, 1880? I've got the right to vote, and I vote to let you out right here."

He held up his hands. "Apology accepted."

I punched him in the shoulder. "That's not a sign of camaraderie. It's a warning."

* * *

Next day we visited Gina's lawyer, Alexander Washington. For once he wasn't on his way to the airport.

Stretching, he propped his feet on the desk and listened intently as we brought him up to speed.

"Yeah, the prosecution and defense have to share raw

evidence with each other before and during the trial. But so far, the cops haven't found all that much, or won't admit it. In cases like this I usually rely on a private investigator."

"We can do that," Stephen said. "Sort of."

"Got a pretty sad track record," I said.

Alexander took a business card from his desk drawer and handed it to me. "This guy is *good*. A little unorthodox, maybe, but he gets the job done."

I read the name. "Kenny Humboldt. *Kenny* sounds . . . immature."

"Some would agree. He's just a little laid back."

"So was the caterpillar in *Alice in Wonderland*."

"Pretty close. Never seen him on mushrooms, though. Maybe a little weed."

"I don't need another semi-conscious millennial partner."

Stephen sat up. "Are you referring to me?"

The lawyer took his feet off the desk. "Like I said, he's exceptional. And busy. Not sure he'll even have time. Say you can't live without him. That usually gets his attention."

He paused. "Oh and tell him he still owes me for that incident with the trombone in St. Louis. He'll know what I'm talking about."

He swung his feet back.

"Well, what are you waiting for?"

* * *

Kenny Humboldt's office was in Greenwich Village, sandwiched between a candle shop and the campaign office of the Socialist Party USA.

After pulling into a pay-for-parking lot, we crossed the street. It was lined with rainbow flags and light poles plastered with posters for medical marijuana shops and concerts headlined by withered flower children.

We climbed a flight of narrow, creaking wooden steps, turned right, and opened a door. HUMBOLDT INVESTIGATIONS, it said, hand-painted in a gold typeface straight out of a fifties *noir* film.

"Reminds me of Raymond Chandler," Stephen said. "*Double Indemnity*. Otto Preminger."

"More like Sam Spade's place, only cleaner."

I took the business card from my purse. My partner followed me inside.

An ancient oak receptionist's desk nearly filled the room. No one sat behind it.

Clearing my throat, I checked my timepiece.

"So far I'm not impressed."

A noise came from somewhere in back. Finally a tall, thin, thirtyish man in a denim outfit and Mets cap sauntered in, hands in his pockets. His hair was curly, blond. His grin was sly. His eyes were of the bedroom variety.

"*Alright*," he said with a wink, then ushered us into his *sanctum sanctorum*. "Whatever your problem, this is the right place."

With a wave he invited us to sit down.

"We can't live without you," Stephen said.

Kenny chuckled. "Don't tell me. You've been listening to Alexander."

"Says you owe him for something involving a trombone in St. Louis," I said.

He put a finger to his lips. "I've been known to be naughty. Sure *he* remembers more clearly what happened. I was somewhat inebriated. Or exploring the wonders of cannabis."

"Now you're just trying to impress me." I slipped the

card back in my purse. Against my better judgment I explained the sort of help we needed.

He stretched lazily in his chair. "Any friend of Alexander's is a friend of mine, especially if you're paying me per diem plus expenses."

"I'm not . . . yet."

"Patience is my greatest virtue, right next to modesty. We'll get your lawyer lady out—God willing, and the creek don't rise." He paused. "Sure she's innocent?"

"Positive."

"Always makes it a little easier."

He took out a yellow legal pad and pen.

"Let's have at 'er."

CHAPTER 27

KENNY CAME AROUND THE FRONT OF HIS DESK, BALANCED on the edge, and picked up the phone. "Gotta make a quick call. Don't take it personally."

Stephen and I looked at each other.

"Alexander? Kenny. I'm here with two new clients. One has reddish hair. The other has legs that won't quit."

"Your hair doesn't look that red to me," Stephen whispered. I could feel my face turning a shade of it.

"They're legit, right?" He put the phone on speaker. "Have the cops shared any physical evidence with you on this Turnbull thing?"

"*Trumbull,*" Alexander said. "There's precious little. Murder weapon, fingerprints."

"Okay. Catch you later."

He hung up. "Need to see the crime scene. Got a key to Trumbull's office?"

"No," I said. "But if we stop by Peggy Van Plugh's on the way, *she* probably does."

Downstairs I started toward the parking lot.

"Oh, let's take *my* car," Kenny said. "Everybody deserves to ride in a custom-painted bronze Lincoln Town car at least once."

"But I'm *paying* to park mine."

"No worries. I know a guy. We'll catch it on the flip flop."

After steering us toward the last row, he pressed the button on his fob. *BEEP*.

Stephen turned toward the source of the sound. "Oh, my God. Never seen anything so shiny."

"I know a car wash guy, too. But that's another story."

On the way Kenny recounted how he'd won the vehicle in a poker game with a Houston oil man. The victim couldn't forgive him, so he'd moved to Greenwich Village. Figured the guy wouldn't come anywhere near a liberal like Susan Sarandon.

When we pulled up to Pendleton House, cars were bumper-to-bumper. Kenny was unfazed. "I'll circle the block 'til you come down."

In the lobby we waved to the guard with the orange glasses. He waved back.

Peggy was at her desk. "Could we borrow the key to Roger's office?" I asked.

She eyed us suspiciously. "Why do you want it?"

"We thought the police might have missed something."

The prospect seemed to make her nervous. Finally, she got it out of her desk and placed it in my palm.

"How long do you need it?"

"Just for tonight. We'll bring it back in the morning."

"This is my only copy. I suppose Maintenance has a couple."

"Thanks."

Back downstairs, we waited until Kenny and his Town Car rounded the corner. There was no missing him.

We climbed in.

"Thought you'd never get here. I'm about running out of gas."

He pulled away from the curb. "Got the key?"

Holding it up, I dangled it over the seat. "Roger's admin didn't want to part with it."

"You thinkin' what I'm thinkin'? Maybe she's afraid you'll find something she left behind."

"Could be."

"Fear's a great motivator. That and the prospect of a five-course Tex-Mex lobster dinner. Which I assume you'll be treating me to later this evening."

I put the key in my purse. "I fear you have my budget confused with your expense account."

He winked at me in the rearview mirror. "Okay, *four* courses. You're holding all the cards."

"Except for the one up your sleeve," I said.

Stephen made a disgusted noise. "Who writes your dialogue?"

"Kenny Rogers' nephew," I said.

* * *

The key worked.

Peggy waited outside. As we entered, I could smell the dust and leather of Roger's law library.

Kenny took off his cap and hung it on a coat hook. "They've got the prints, so we don't need gloves. Maybe hair from the carpet. Let's divide the room three ways like a pecan pie, and—"

"You'd eat a third of a pie yourself?" Stephen asked. "Man, we have more in common than I thought."

"What I mean is stick to your territory." He stepped off the imaginary boundaries.

I got most of the shelves. Opening books, I searched for stuck-in notes and hollowed-out volumes.

Stephen was assigned the window side, with a globe on a stand and six filing cabinets.

Kenny reserved the desk, chairs, and an antique pump organ. Roger must have loved old things, which explained why he'd dated me.

Stephen sat down and began to play what sounded a little like *Stairway to Heaven.* Hard to tell, since he and the organ were wheezing in unison.

"Stick to your knitting," Kenny said. "Look at all those juicy files."

Mumbling, Stephen slunk back to his side of the room.

I came upon several uninformative bookmarks and no hollow volumes. But a few slips of paper caught my attention. One was inserted at the beginning of a case involving employment law.

Kenny whistled. Turning, we saw him hold up something round and white.

"Found it in the desk," he said. "Guess what it is."

I squinted. "Can't tell."

"Too small for a billiard ball," Stephen said.

Mr. Laid-Back raised his eyebrows. "Glass eye." He brought it close to his own.

"Can't believe the police missed it," I said.

He placed it on the blotter. "Probably didn't. Not a weapon. Paper clips would be more dangerous."

"Why would he have a glass eye in his desk?" Stephen asked.

Kenny looked me. "You went out with him, right? Did he have a glass eye?"

"How would I know?"

"He'd have that thing going that Sammy Davis, Sandy Duncan, and Peter Falk did. Kind of wanders off in its own direction."

"Then I'd say no."

"Although I guess they have much better fakes these days. Probably couldn't tell."

He examined the vitreous orb again. "What was Mr. Trumbull's eye color?"

I thought for a moment. "Green. Sort of hazel."

He brought it over to give me a closer look.

"Yeah, something like that."

He put the eye in his pocket and pulled out his phone.

"What was that detective's number?"

"Uh . . . 555-9673."

He dialed and put the phone on speaker. Took three minutes for him to charm Spiner into checking the autopsy report for any mention of a glass eye. I didn't think it was possible.

Finally, the detective said, "Negative. No mention of an ocular prosthesis."

"Thank you, my dear," Kenny said, and hung up.

He scratched his chin. "Huh. So, whose is it? And why is it in his desk?"

* * *

On the way back to my car, we stopped for dinner. To Kenny's disappointment I picked a Captain D's restaurant.

"All you've got so far is questions," I said. "With answers you get lobster."

They got the Ultimate Seafood Platter. I ordered the Seafood Gumbo, reminding myself that okra is a vegetable—though an inedible one.

We were halfway through when Kenny leaned back and dabbed at his lips with his napkin. "Any of our suspects have a glass eye?"

Stephen and I looked at each other.

"No idea," I said. "Either way, why would the murderer leave it in the desk? As some kind of calling card, like a serial killer?"

Kenny folded his arms. "Maybe it doesn't belong to the murderer. What if he or she stole it and left it behind to incriminate somebody else? Somebody who *does* wear a glass eye?"

"Or somebody who was very, *very* close to him and left it there as a spare. And no, it wasn't me."

Stephen took a last bite of his fish and burped delicately. "Or maybe the eyeball was a good luck charm."

"Of all the publishing houses in the world, you had to walk into mine," I said.

"So we need to find out who the eye belongs to," Kenny said.

"Or who made it. Or both."

He took the thing from his pocket and spun it on the table. "Too bad nobody signed it."

"Must be a way to ID it," I said.

Stephen tried a little spinning himself, but the orb flew off the table. "There was a cop who tracked a bank robber by matching the bite marks on a teller's wrist with the guy's dental records. Put him away for six years, but he chewed his way out." He reached down and picked up the glass eye. "Saw it on *Mindhunter*." After popping a butterfly shrimp in his mouth, he looked at Kenny and smiled.

"Remember when I said I couldn't live without you?" he asked. "I take it back."

CHAPTER 28

NEXT DAY WE MET AT KENNY'S OFFICE TO LIST THE suspects whose eyeballs—or eyeball-making skills—we needed to examine.

He lacked a whiteboard. "Used to have two, but one night after sampling a particularly fine specimen of Purple Kush, I accidentally used a permanent marker. That solvent enhanced the experience, but the boards were beyond repair."

We used a yellow legal pad instead. Kenny asked me to take notes.

"I'm not your secretary. Take a hike."

He shrugged. "I'd put the martial-arts chick at the top, mainly 'cause of her physical strength. Bruce Lee had one eye. Not many people know that."

Stephen did a facepalm. "Are you kidding? He had *three*. One was invisible, in the middle of his forehead."

I tossed the pad in the center of the table. "Enough. We've got Elaine Jeong. And of course Martin Curry. He's got to have enough artificial body parts to make him bionic."

Kenny took the pad and tapped his pen on it. "What's the secretary's name?"

"Peggy Van Plugh."

"Didn't you say she looked nervous about giving you the key?"

"I did."

Stephen raised a hand. "And Liza Boxer. I think she's got a crush on me."

"More of an obsession," I said. "And she's a regular Martha Stewart when it comes to arts and crafts. Maybe she's figured out how to sell her glass eyes on Pinterest."

"I'll look it up."

Kenny scribbled on the pad. "How about—Gina, is it?"

"She looks you right in the eye. Except when she's sleeping. Far as I'm concerned, she shouldn't be on the list at all."

He added up the names. "Makes four. I vote we hit the road and find them."

Stephen quit poking his phone. "Found Liza's Pinterest account. Don't see any glass eyes. Seems to make a mean knitted toilet roll cover, though. Oughtta get me one."

Kenny tore the page from his pad, stuffed it in his pocket, and put on his cap. "You're a lucky man. I've dallied with my share of ladies, but none quite so domesticated."

Fishing the eye from his pocket again, he proceeded to spin it on the desk like a roulette wheel's ball. "Where it stops, nobody knows."

* * *

We tried Peggy next. She was out of the office.

But Martin Curry was there—back at work, using a cane.

He looked warily at Kenny. "I've seen you before. Just can't remember where."

Kenny showed him the glass eye. "This yours?"

"Nope. Wrong color."

"So you *have* one of these marbles?"

He pointed to his left eye. "Son, I've had a collection of 'em since before you were born. Used to have wooden teeth like George Washington. And don't get me started on my gutta-percha nose, the screws in my hip, and the plate in my head."

"You have any idea why Roger had a glass eye in his desk?" I asked.

"None whatsoever. But he was an odd fellow, wasn't he?"

"How so?"

"I'd rather not speak ill of the dead—seeing I'll soon be among them." He smiled, then caned himself out and down the hall.

"Well, that was productive," Stephen said.

Breaking for lunch at the cafeteria, I wondered aloud what Martin meant about Roger being odd.

"Takes one to know one," Kenny said.

Next was Elaine Jeong. We called first to find out where she was, but just got her voicemail.

I called Liza Boxer.

"I'm at the Post Office," she said. "Mailing my orders of handmade popcorn balls."

"Mind if we join you?"

"The more the merrier. I'm at the one on Federal Plaza."

Half an hour later, we were still standing in line with her. Kenny held up the glass eye.

"Oooh," she breathed. "The workmanship is *beautiful.*"

"Ever made any of these?" I asked.

"Tried to blow glass *ornaments* once, but I burned myself." She showed off a scar on her arm, just above her brace.

"And you don't wear a glass eye yourself?"

She giggled. Nobody laughed.

She blushed. "Not that it's funny. I just—never mind."

Finally we reached the head of the line.

"Anything else?" Liza asked Stephen, batting her eyelashes.

He looked squeamish. "Get the insurance. That's about it."

Back in the car, Kenny laughed, "Man, she's got it *bad* for you."

"Feeling's not mutual, dude."

"One to go," Kenny said, crossing her name off the list.

I tried Peggy again, and this time connected. "I'm at The Cryogenic Castle." I put her on speaker.

"Is that in Disney World?"

"No, it's on Columbus Avenue. They put you in a freezing chamber that makes you burn calories and boost your metabolism."

"That explains why your teeth are chattering."

"So can this wait?"

"It won't take long."

She sighed. "I should be out in twenty minutes."

"We'll be there."

I hung up. "Rather die from obesity than subject myself to that."

We met her in the lobby. She was a startling shade of periwinkle.

"Follow my finger," I said.

She shivered but managed to do it.

Kenny went through the routine of showing her the glass eye and asking why Roger had it in his desk.

"Didn't know he had it. Can't imagine why. But he did a lot of things I couldn't explain."

"Name one," Kenny said.

She hesitated. "Well, he had this habit of looking in the mirror and whispering to himself."

Kenny raised an eyebrow.

"He also liked taking credit for other people's achievements. He did that several times with Gina, and she never questioned it or complained. Does that help?"

"You bet."

We got up to leave. The receptionist, slender as an icicle, came over and gave me a card. "Twenty percent off your first visit."

Smiling through gritted teeth, I handed it to Stephen.

* * *

Back at Kenny's office, he took out the glass eye once more.

He and Stephen played a sort of foosball game, flicking it back and forth across the desk.

"So, whatcha think?" Kenny asked, not looking up.

"Not sure the glass eye's going to be our Magic 8-Ball," I said. "But now we know Roger had something strange going on."

Stephen glanced up. The eyeball dropped to the carpet. "How do we find out what it was?"

Kenny scooped up the sightless sphere. "Did Roger have any living family members?"

"Told me he had an older sister in Queens," I said.

"Retired teacher or something. Funny, I don't remember meeting her at the funeral. Maybe they didn't get along."

Stephen pulled out his phone. "I'm on it."

CHAPTER 29

I HELD OUT MY HAND TO KENNY. "I'LL TAKE THE EYE."

"But it's so much fun to play with."

"I think it belongs in Roger's office. Also, it seems like some kind of Egyptian amulet that curses whoever disturbs it."

"You've been watching too many mummy movies."

I snapped my fingers. "Just give it here, all right?"

He shrugged and tossed it my way. Into my purse it went.

Stephen held up his phone. "I've found four female Trumbulls in Queens."

After writing down the numbers and calling the first, I got voicemail. Didn't leave a message.

Somebody answered the second call, but it was a man. Chumbawamba's "Tubthumping" throbbed in the background.

I switched to speaker. "I'm looking for Roger Trumbull's sister."

"You mean Anne?"

"Uh, sure."

"Hey, Annie! Phone for you." The music stopped.

"Yeah?" said a woman's voice.

"This is Caroline Neville. Friend of your brother."

"That makes one of us."

Ouch. Sibling rivalry confirmed.

"We're trying to find out who killed him. Could we come by and—"

"I'm in the middle of something."

"I mean tomorrow."

She sighed. "Fine. Ten o'clock?"

"Perfect. Thank you. And I'm sorry for your—"

The phone went dead.

"Loss," I added.

"Nice work," Stephen said. "Got her on the second try."

"Sounds grief-stricken, doesn't she?"

Kenny took out a clipper and worked on his nails. "Must be in the last stage. Apathy."

* * *

Next morning, Stephen and I parked near a brownstone on 227th Avenue in Jamaica, a middle-class neighborhood.

Kenny zipped past in his Lincoln Town Car and found another space.

When we got to the door, we heard more loud music.

"Weezer," said Stephen.

"My, my," Kenny drawled. "How old *is* this lady?"

"Here's a tip," I said. "Don't ask her."

A sixtyish man in a tank-top undershirt and jeans opened the door. Had more chest hair than Brad Garrett.

"Annie!" he yelled. The music stopped.

A bony, seventyish woman with braided gray hair

and wearing a tie-dyed bathrobe emerged from the kitchen.

"Pardon my looks. Don't get dressed until noon. Played enough dress-up when I was a teacher."

I handled introductions.

Her overage boyfriend left the room, scratching himself.

We sat down. Kenny picked up a copy of *High Times* magazine. "My kind of lady," he said, training his smile on Annie.

"What did you teach?" I asked.

"Home economics. Coached the cheerleaders. Subbed 'til last year. Got sick of trying to keep the animals in line."

"We're stuck trying to find Roger's killer."

"Thought they caught her. The lawyer. Had the knife and everything."

I nodded. "I know the lady. She couldn't possibly have done it."

Kenny leaned forward, palms on his knees. "Annie, we keep hearing that Roger was a little eccentric. You knew him pretty well. Ring true?"

She turned to the table next to the couch and tapped a Camel from its pack. "Didn't see much of him the last ten years or so. Didn't get along when we were kids, either. Always the teacher's pet, the class president, the one who watched *Jeopardy* every night and answered the questions the second they came out of Alex Trebek's mouth. Frankly, I miss Alex more than I miss Roger."

After lighting the cigarette she took a puff. "My brother was a little obsessed with appearance. Talked to himself. These days they'd call him compulsive or a bit schizophrenic. But it never slowed him down. Probably made twenty times what I did."

"Did these things ever get him in trouble?"

"He took credit for other people's work, and it made him some enemies. Might say he was a user. Manipulator. From what I've read in the paper, a couple of women who worked for him were pretty ticked off—including the one they arrested."

"So we've heard."

She took another draw on the cigarette and flicked the ash into a mug with the Brooklyn Bridge on it. "There was that time in high school when he was going with a girl who thought he hung the stars. After about a year, he dumped her. Didn't tell her in person, just over the phone. Took up with another one, a Queens city councilman's daughter. Always had political aspirations. Probably figured it was a good career move. Would have made a fine congressman or something. Phony as could be."

She pointed her cigarette at Kenny. "Like *this* one."

Kenny bowed. "You flatter me."

She checked her watch. "Any more questions? *The View* is on pretty soon."

I thought for a moment. "We found a glass eye in Roger's desk. Any idea why it might be there?"

She coughed. "Dad had a glass eye. Family heirloom, I guess. The old man didn't leave us much else. I got his dentures."

I got up. "Well, that solves *one* mystery."

Kenny touched Annie lightly on the cheek. "You really ought to give up those coffin nails. Smoking's bad for you—tobacco, at least."

She picked up the remote and turned on the TV. "If I were thirty years younger, I'd lead you on myself. Just so I could break your heart."

Kenny grinned. "If we were forty years older, I'd let you."

* * *

Outside we gathered around my car.

"Interesting lady," Kenny said.

I opened the door. "Think we're narrowing it down. Which of our suspects, other than Gina, have reason to feel let down, misused, or led on?"

"Peggy and Liza," Stephen answered. "Women scorned."

"A bit sexist, but true. Let's move them higher up the list."

"How do we get them to open up?"

I nodded toward Kenny. "If Mr. Charm here can't do it, there's always a compassionate editor who understands women."

Stephen shrugged. "Hey, what can I say? It comes naturally."

"I was thinking of me."

"So was I."

CHAPTER 30

BACK AT THE OFFICE WE FOUND PEGGY, CONSIDERABLY rosier than she'd been after coming out of the freezer.

She sat at her desk, facing a tubby, bearded, balding quadragenarian in a vested suit. A Kit Kat wrapper stuck out of his pocket.

She introduced him. "Roger's replacement. Bellamy Lazar. We're doing a little orientation."

I nodded. "We've met, at least over the phone." I'd tried to get his opinions on consent forms and contract breaches, a seemingly eternal process akin to prying rivets from a pot-bellied stove with a letter opener.

"Afraid I don't remember *you*," he said, eyelids at half-mast.

Not bothering to tell him our names, Peggy faced him again. "So much for putting callers on hold. Now on to the stapler."

"I know how to do that."

"This one's electric."

She scooped a pile of papers from a wastebasket and

demonstrated. The thing went *POW*, like a roofer's nail gun. His eyes widened.

"Now *you* try," she commanded.

"Is there a safety?"

"No. Just pick the thing up. Not going to bite you."

He held it as if preparing to defuse a bomb. Leaning over the desk, he tore a thin sheaf of papers from her stack and positioned the weapon. He squeezed it so hard his hand trembled. Then *POW*.

Somehow he managed to anchor his tie to the desk calendar.

Peggy closed her eyes. "Anyone have a pair of pliers?"

Chubby was starting to breathe hard, his face reddening. He tried to stand up, but the staple had embedded itself in the wood.

"Your instructions weren't specific," he said. "You didn't say how hard to push."

Kenny ambled over and grabbed the tie. "Hold still." He yanked. Lazar squeaked, then straightened up.

Peggy opened her eyes.

"We need to talk," I said. She looked as if I'd thrown her a lifesaver.

Roger's replacement waddled back into his office, trying to work the steel out of the fabric.

I pulled Kenny over. "This is Mr. Humboldt. A private detective who's helping Gina."

He bent over and kissed her hand.

Producing a squeak of her own, Peggy pulled her hand away as if he'd licked it.

He seemed surprised, but only for an instant. "Ma'am, I've never seen such a tidy office. I wonder whether you'd do me the honor of dropping by my humble abode sometime and putting everything in its place. Except me, of course."

She appeared to have sunk her fangs into a bitter lemon.

"Did any of Roger's oddities make you think he needed professional help?" he asked.

Picking up a stray law book, she shelved it. "No, I think not. We all have our quirks, don't we?"

"Did he make you feel uncomfortable? Scared?"

"No, of course not." She put the stapler back in the desk.

I took Kenny and Stephen aside. "Charm's not going to cut it," I whispered. "Have to get her to admit how angry she is about the way Roger treated her."

"Good luck with *that*," Stephen mumbled.

"Let's all sit down, shall we?" Peggy looked suspicious but did it anyway.

"What did your note say?" I asked.

"What note?"

"The one to Roger. About leading you on."

"I don't remember."

"Did you keep a copy?"

"No."

"What did Roger say when he read it?"

"That I was imagining things. Then he tore it up."

She shifted uncomfortably in her chair. Her left hand balled into a fist.

"Why'd you say it was a forgery? Who would do that?"

"I don't know. Maybe Gina."

"Come on. She had no reason to."

Her right hand matched the left. "For all I know, she wanted Roger for herself. He was an attractive man. Apparently *you* thought so."

I ignored the jab. "Did he ever acknowledge all you did to keep things running?"

"No."

"Ever promote you?"

She stood. "Are you kidding?"

"A raise, maybe?"

She ground her high heel into the carpet. "He treated me like dirt, all right?"

"Is that why you killed him and planted the knife in Gina's purse?"

"*What?* I did no such thing!"

For a moment it looked as if she might throttle me. "I know you're Gina's friend, but you must be desperate to even *suggest* that."

I picked up my purse. "I can see you're upset. I'd be, too, if somebody treated me that way."

I rose to my feet. "We'll show ourselves out."

Kenny and Stephen followed.

She stood there, trembling.

The door behind her opened. Lazar lumbered back in.

"Are you any good at fixing ties?"

"No!"

Without a word he shrank back and returned to his office.

* * *

Back in the car, Kenny let out a *Whoa*.

"If I hadn't seen it with my own eyes, I wouldn't believe you had it in you."

"Just doing my job."

"Figure she won't be stopping by to smarten up my office anytime soon."

I started the car. "Stephen, would you call Liza to make sure she's home?"

After getting her on the line, he hit SPEAKER. She sounded breathless.

"Just made a batch of toffee bars and can't wait for you to try them."

"Can I bring a couple of friends?"

"Anybody I know?"

"You know *half* of them."

"What do you like to drink with toffee bars?"

"Old Milwaukee Light."

"Got lemonade. Out of bilk."

"See you soon." He hung up.

When Liza opened the door, I smelled something wonderful. Stephen wiped a little drool from the corner of his mouth.

"I tell you," Kenny whispered, "you can't let this one get away."

"Just watch me. Eventually."

After I introduced Kenny and she served the refreshments, Liza sat on the couch and waited for compliments.

"Three thumbs up," Stephen said.

"You're so sweet."

Leaning toward me, Kenny whispered. "We might as well skip the charm and go directly to merciless interrogation."

"We?"

"Well, it's probably more your style than mine."

I took a napkin and wiped the chocolate off my fingers. "Liza, how many times have you been fired?"

She looked surprised, then irritated. "Three. All of them totally unfair."

"So it wasn't the first time when Mr. Trumbull did it."

"That's what I said."

"Was he right in saying you spent all your time on the Internet and not enough doing research?"

"Of course not. He was prejudiced. Wasn't around enough to even know what I was doing."

Taking another toffee bar, Stephen nodded at me in approval.

"On a scale of one to ten," I continued, "how mad were you when you had to clean out your desk and get ushered out of the building by security?"

"How mad would *you* be?"

"Pretty mad. Were you angry enough to stab him and put the knife in Gina Casebeer's purse?"

Liza sat there, mouth open. "What kind of person do you think I *am?* Besides, I couldn't stab anybody." She held up her arm with the brace.

"Yes, we know about carpal tunnel syndrome. By the way, who's your doctor?"

She hesitated. "Dr. Crane at Rockdale Medical Clinic. But he's not there anymore. I went on the Internet and got the brace myself. It really helps. Not that you care."

"I *do* care. And thank you for the toffee bars."

Stephen wrapped one more in a napkin and stuffed it in his pocket.

Kenny patted Liza on the arm—the braceless one. She recoiled as if he were a rattler.

"You know the way to a man's heart," he said.

"Through the left coronary artery, isn't it?"

For once he was speechless.

* * *

Storm clouds were congregating as we returned to the car. Leaves were rattling in the wind.

"Don't remember the weatherman saying anything about rain," I said.

Stephen held out his hand as if to catch the first drop. "They never get the forecast right."

"Got an umbrella in the trunk." I pulled it out and gave it to him.

The first drops hit as we climbed into the car. They were big and warm and sounded like hail.

"Man, what a downpour," Kenny said. "Almost as bad as Port Arthur, Texas."

We sat there. Visibility was more or less zero. Lightning flashed in the west.

Kenny looked out his window. "Dr. Crane, eh? How convenient that he's moved on."

Stephen fumbled the toffee bar from his pocket and took a bite. "You think the carpal tunnel's real?"

I shrugged. "If it is, how can she knead dough and lift all those pans from the oven? And have you ever tried knitting? Nothing *but* repetitive motion."

Thunder boomed—so close Stephen jumped a little.

"Let's say for the sake of argument that Ms. Boxer is faking it," I said. "That she pulled a knife on Roger. How do we get her to show her hand?"

"So to speak," said Kenny.

"Get Liza to arm wrestle with Peggy," Stephen suggested.

I flopped back in the seat. "No, really."

"I'm serious."

"Seriously *ill.*"

I sighed. "Both have motive and opportunity. What we need is some kind of physical evidence that one of them was there when Roger died. Or an eyewitness."

"To the murder?"

"Not likely. Just somebody who saw one of them

enter Pendleton House." Thunder again, this time more of a *CRRAAACK*.

"There's at least one security camera," Stephen said.

I checked my watch. "Who's at the front desk today, do you think?"

"Probably the old guy with the white mustache and orange-tinted glasses from 1970."

I started the car and the windshield wipers. The rain was still pelting. I could make out trees, swaying in the gale.

"Stephen, can you find pictures of Peggy and Liza?"

"For the guard?"

"Of course. Liza's probably got her face plastered all over Pinterest. Peggy might be on the Pendleton website. I think she was employee of the month, right after Roger died."

He took out his phone. "Battery's dead."

Kenny found his and passed it to Stephen. "Password is Cool Hand Luke."

CHAPTER 31

BY THE TIME WE REACHED THE OFFICE, THE RAIN WAS JUST drizzle. We piled out of the car.

I got the umbrella out of the trunk. When I opened it, two steel ribs popped through the yellow fabric. After closing it I tossed it back in.

Inside the lobby the old guy was sitting on a folding chair next to the reception desk, reading *Popular Science*.

Trying to read the name on his badge, I squinted. LEE.

"Oh, Lee! Hi!"

He looked up. Wished I'd paid more attention all those times I'd passed him.

Cradling the magazine in his lap, he pointed in my direction. "I remember you. You're the one who ignored the CAUTION WET FLOOR sign last Tuesday morning, slipped, and fell on her can."

Stephen and Kenny turned away, snickering.

I put on a smile. "So glad you have such a sharp memory."

"For a man of my age? Is *that* what you mean?"

"Not at all." Pausing, I searched the walls and ceiling. "We have at least one camera trained on this entrance, right?"

"Two, actually."

"Can you retrieve the tapes or disks or whatever they are for the last month or so?"

Bending forward, he lowered his voice. "Don't let it get around, but the cameras have been busted for the last thirty days. Keep asking for replacements, but nobody listens. Guess they think crooks will assume the things still work."

I turned to Stephen. "Find any pictures?"

He pulled them up.

"Lee, do you recognize either of these women?"

He took the phone and adjusted his glasses. "See this one all the time," he said, pointing at Peggy. "Always in a big hurry."

He paused. "This other one I'm not—" He scratched his head. "Yeah, I've seen her, but not for a while. She get fired or something?"

"Exactly. Now, this is harder. Do you recall whether either of them came through here any time after four o'clock on March 18?"

He snorted. "Lady, if I were still in my *twenties,* I couldn't tell you that."

"It was a Friday. The lobby was still decorated for St. Patrick's Day."

He closed his eyes. For a moment I thought he'd fallen asleep.

Finally, his eyelids snapped open. "I could be wrong. But it seems to me the first one hustled out just before five with two of those sparkly green leprechaun hats under her arm, like there'd just been a party."

"How about the other one?"

"She was on her way in a few minutes later, carrying a brown paper bag. Couldn't tell what was in it, of course." He handed the phone back.

For a moment I wanted to kiss him, but his toothbrush mustache killed the urge quickly. "You're amazing."

"So I'm told," he said, and went back to reading.

* * *

I glanced through the front windows. Lightning flared in the distance, but the rain had stopped.

"Well, *that* clears things up," Kenny drawled.

"Are we talking about the weather?"

"Uh-uh. Now we got two of our most likely suspects on the scene at about the same time."

"Wonder whether the old man's testimony would hold up in court."

"Depends on whether the prosecution can make him look feeble. I'd put my money on *him*."

My phone rang. It was Spiner.

She got right to the point.

"Martin Curry's confessed to the murder."

* * *

I told Stephen and Kenny what had happened.

"Curry?" Kenny asked, looking confused.

"She's gotta be kidding," said Stephen.

I put the phone on speaker.

"Hard to take him seriously," the detective said, "but his fingerprints are all over Trumbull's desk. If this is his idea of a joke, it's not very funny."

"Maybe it's dementia," I said.

"Whatever it is, we have to follow up. Hate to waste the taxpayers' money, but you have to track down every lead, no matter how stupid. God knows I learned *that* the hard way."

I told her about Peggy and Liza.

"Nice. Maybe they *both* did it. I'll talk to the D.A.'s office about the security guard."

"You'll love him."

"In the meantime, stay dry. They're predicting one of those storm-of-the-century things before the week's over. Gotta go." The line went dead.

"Last time that happened," Stephen said, "power was out for two or three days. Blackouts from the Bronx to Staten Island. Bunch of babies born nine months later."

"Just what we need," I said.

CHAPTER 32

I DECIDED WE HAD TO CLEAR UP THE QUESTION: WHY would Martin confess to a crime nobody thought he could have committed?

When I called Kenny the next morning, he had another case to work on. "Let me know when you two run out of charm," he said.

Stephen and I returned to the office. We found Martin poking Peggy between the shoulder blades with his cane.

His eyes twinkled. "Guess who's back?"

"Keep that up and I swear I'll call Security," she said.

He scoffed. "That old guy with the giant glasses? I could take him in two rounds with my *tuchus* tied behind my back."

"Not medically possible," Stephen said.

When Peggy saw us, she frowned and stood up. "Another ambush? I'm on break. You can spend some quality time with Henny Youngman here." Taking a manila envelope from her desk, she shoved it under her arm and left.

Martin smiled. Planting his cane on the floor, he sank slowly onto the couch. "No sense of humor. In my day, whenever that was, that line would kill at Grossinger's."

He waited for a reaction, which nobody provided. "Resort hotel in the Catskills. Did my first show there in the winter of '52. The artificial snow didn't fool anybody."

Stephen and I sat. "Martin," I said, "we just heard the most unbelievable rumor."

"It's a lie. I'm not pregnant." He paused. "Holding for laughs."

"Why in the world would you confess to killing Roger? You obviously couldn't have stabbed him. And what's with the fingerprints all over his desk?"

He picked up his cane and rolled the shaft between his fingers. "Who says I couldn't stab him? I have the strength of ten Jews full of Manischewitz. And he never gave me credit for anything. The same way he treated Gina."

"What about the fingerprints?"

"I came in one day when Roger was gone and sat in his chair for a while. *Tremendous* back support, I'll tell you. Got myself a cup of coffee and managed to spill a little on the desk. I was wiping it up with a napkin when His Majesty walked in." He stamped his cane on the floor. "Such language you wouldn't *believe*."

He paused. "Told me if I ever touched his desk again he'd fire me. Next morning, before he came in . . . Well, you can imagine the rest."

"How did Roger treat Gina?"

"Like a dog treats a fire hydrant."

"Are you trying to take the rap for her? You wouldn't last six months in prison."

"Probably less, given my boyish good looks. But I

won't last that long *out* of prison, either. Gina still has some tread on her. And I've always . . . well . . ."

"Had a crush on her?"

"What am I, Archie from the comics? Let's just say she doesn't deserve to spend the rest of her life sleeping on a concrete slab and eating expired pastrami."

I tried another tack. "Before you confessed, did you talk to a lawyer?"

"I *am* a lawyer."

"Did you sign anything?"

"Sure."

"You can recant a confession, right?"

"If you want, but it sounds pretty suspicious. It's not like they were beating me with nightsticks."

"I'll have to tell the detective about this, you know."

"Tell her what? I didn't admit anything. You and I were just having a nice conversation, the two of us."

He glanced at Stephen. "Three."

I got up. "You're one in a million, you know that?"

"Thank God. If there were more of me, the jails would be full, and the synagogues would be empty." Tapping his silver-eagle-headed cane on my forehead, he smiled.

* * *

In the car I tried three times to call Gina.

Third was the charm. She sounded tired as usual, but this time kept coughing and apologizing.

"Been to the infirmary?" I asked.

"They said it was bronchitis. Gave me an antibiotic. I'm sure you can tell it's *very* effective."

I told her about Martin's confession.

Gina sniffed. "I had no idea he felt that way. Always the clown. But I can't let him do this. He'd *die* in prison."

"Don't worry. There's no hard evidence to back him up. Unfortunately, there's too much against *you*. But we're looking into a couple of your fellow employees who also have motive and opportunity. And a lot more temperament."

"Who?"

"Peggy and Liza."

She coughed again. "No argument here. So what are you going to do?"

"Try to convince a certain detective to keep an open mind."

She cleared her throat. "Good luck."

"You too." I hung up and started the car.

"Don't tell me," Stephen said. "I know where we're going." Leaning against the headrest, he closed his eyes.

"And I can guess why."

* * *

Another rainstorm rolled in from the north. The top of the Empire State Building was lost in the clouds.

I called Spiner to make sure she'd be there.

"I'm two miles from the station. Fatal carjacking."

After getting directions, I flipped the wipers to the three-dot mark. Cars were starting to hydroplane.

Pulling into traffic and stopping at a light, I narrowly avoided getting rear-ended.

We had to park three blocks away. I got out the umbrella despite its condition. Stephen joined me under its pathetic excuse for protection.

Amid flashing lights, we spotted Spiner. Her leather

coat was covered by a clear plastic poncho. She hailed us. "Wait in the bus stop!"

After we dripped for three minutes, she tiptoed over through the mud. "So, what's this about?"

I boiled the conversation with Martin down to the essentials.

She nodded. "Yeah, he signed the confession, but nobody's going to take it seriously. Least of all me. Still think this is a sign of losing his marbles."

Folding up the remains of my broken bumbershoot, I dropped it in the trash can.

"Talked to the D.A.'s office about the security guy," she continued. "All subject to change, but there's a chance they could put him on the stand. They'll want to vet him first."

"And the two women in Trumbull's office?"

"I can't haul them in on suspicion of murder. We could question them, but they'll just get lawyers. We need a heck of a lot more. Too bad they're not into confessions, but most real perpetrators aren't."

"How much is 'a heck of a lot'?"

"More than *you've* got."

CHAPTER 33

STEPHEN AND I SLOGGED BACK TO THE CAR.

"You smell like a wet dog," I said.

"So do you."

I asked him to take out his phone. "We need to set up a meeting. Get all the suspects together. Just a few more puzzle pieces and I'll be ready."

He opened his door and got in. "Do we *have* to do this like Agatha Christie? Can't we just figure things out and let Spiner arrest somebody?"

I got in on my side. "We have to get at least one person to tell the truth. Maybe incriminate somebody else. Being in the same room puts pressure on everybody."

We headed toward Pendleton House. Lightning seemed to be striking all around us. A tree in a park was hit, sending a shower of sparks to the ground.

Stephen activated his phone. "Can't get people together on the spur of the moment. It's almost seven o'clock."

"Try."

I flipped the wipers to maximum. At the next intersection the signals were out. I slowed to a crawl. Nobody was coming, so I kept going.

Every traffic light was out for the next 20 blocks or so. Windows were still lit in the skyscrapers.

After parking we dashed into the building.

The old guy with big glasses glanced up from his magazine and gave us a wave.

The elevators being out, we took the stairs to my office. Looking out the window, we could see lights winking off like fireflies in a sandstorm.

"Can't get anybody out in this weather," I said. "Can you make it a Zoom meeting?"

"*I* can. But how many of our suspects know which end of a computer is up?"

I tore yesterday's page from my *Dilbert* desk calendar, turned it over, and started making a list. "Elaine Jeong. Liza and Peggy. Martin."

Switching chairs, he fired up my laptop. "I can tell you right now Martin Curry would do better with a telegraph key than a computer."

"Maybe not in a storm like this. Martin can use a telephone. Try patching him in or something."

I picked up my desk phone and called Martin, then explained my plan.

"I don't know from Zoom. I'm in the middle of eating a kosher TV dinner and watching a *Love Boat*."

"Lucky your power's not out."

"I'll sit by the phone and wait. Ray Milland's in this one. My God, what an actor."

"We'll call you back."

Next was Elaine. She was breathing heavily, as if she'd been working out. When she heard my proposal, she told me exactly where to go.

"Not today, thanks. But if you're the only one who doesn't show, it'll look pretty suspicious, don't you think?"

"Who else is going to be there?"

"Everybody who's somebody."

"Don't expect me to put on a happy face."

"Never. Wouldn't want you to hurt yourself." I hung up.

"Now Liza and Peggy." I found their numbers.

I got Liza's voicemail, but she picked up at the last second.

"Hello?"

"This is Carolyn Neville. Do you know how to do a—"

"*You* again?"

I went over my plan.

She cleared her throat. "I'm going to put down the phone and count to ten."

I waited.

"Centered now," she said.

"I'm sure you've got nothing to hide. And you'd have the pleasure of watching some people you don't care for squirm."

"Since you put it that way, I'm in."

"We'll call back."

Peggy answered right away. When she heard my voice, there was a click—then nothing.

I tried again. "Don't hang up," I said when she answered.

"It's not what you think," I continued. "Just a little virtual get-together. Sort of a party. BYOB. Maybe even make your case for staying out of jail. Up to you."

She sighed. "Zoom or FaceTime?"

"Zoom."

"When?"

"Soon as we can set it up."

Thunder rumbled again. "Hope your laptop is charged," I said.

"Whatever." The line went dead.

I reached Detective Spiner. She was in her cubicle, filing a report on the carjacking. "Yeah, I can do Zoom. Hate it, but I can do it."

I read her the guest list.

"You must be pretty persuasive. Or a good liar."

"I'd like to think the former."

"I'll be here." More thunder echoed in the background before she hung up.

I put the phone down. "Just one more, and we can—"

Suddenly the overhead fluorescents buzzed and flickered out. By the time I my eyes got accustomed to the dark, the weaker safety lights kicked in.

Stephen looked up. "Hope the generator holds out. And our batteries."

He peered at the laptop. "Sixty-two percent power."

"Got forty-nine on my phone. We should be good."

I looked at my list. "Is that everybody?"

"Shouldn't Kenny be in on this?"

"Guess so. Will he fit on the screen? His head's pretty big."

"We all should. If we do it right."

I dialed Kenny.

"Miss me?" he asked. "Certainly missed you."

I told him what we were arranging.

He cackled. "You want to get them raving or blubbering like a witness on *Matlock?*"

"Entertaining, but not necessary."

"Well, remember the honey and vinegar thing. I'll be glad to supply the honey."

"Don't call us. We'll call you."

I pressed END.

* * *

We could hear the wind whistle, even through the windows. Raindrops pelted the glass like rubber bullets.

I checked my watch. "Seven-thirty. Curtain time."

I got Martin on his landline, then called the others.

Elaine appeared first on the laptop screen, sitting too far away to be heard.

"Can you get closer?" Stephen called.

She rolled her desk chair forward. A white Russian wolfhound paced to and fro in the background, then nuzzled her elbow. Frowning, she stroked him or her.

Detective Spiner tuned in, drinking coffee and scribbling on her report.

All at once Liza popped onto the screen, way too close and blurry.

I leaned in. "Liza, can you move back a bit?"

She pushed her chair back and adjusted her brace.

Kenny's out-of-focus hand appeared in the middle of the Brady Bunch grid, then went lower.

He grinned. "Hey, hey, hey. I can see y'all. Y'all see me?"

"Yes," I said.

Peggy was last, perfectly framed. No beer, no smile. A cat, ginger tabby, sat in her lap.

"Thanks for coming," I said. "Martin Curry's joined us on the phone, so you won't see him."

The detective looked up from her report. "Mr. Curry, I know you confessed, but—"

Peggy leaned forward. "Martin *confessed?*"

Liza gasped.

Spiner cleared her throat. "But I know he didn't do it."

He wheezed into the phone. "I take that as an insult."

"Take it any way you like. If you want to be thrown into prison, you'll have to commit an actual *crime*."

Nose in the air, he hung up.

I checked the laptop's charge. Still okay.

"Ms. Jeong, that's a beautiful dog."

"Yeah, but get to the point."

Kenny winked. "You're one powerful lady. I like that in a woman."

"You're one sleazy moron. I hate that in a man."

Kenny looked startled. "Be that as it may, it took one strong woman to stab poor Mr. Trumbull to death."

She gave a bronx cheer. "Anybody with five fingers could have done it."

I turned to Peggy. "Something you should know. We have an eyewitness who'll testify that he saw you leave just before five with a couple of green hats under your arm."

"That's a lie."

"And you, Liza. The same person saw you on your way in just after that, carrying a brown paper bag."

"No way."

All at once the laptop screen froze. Stephen rubbed the trackpad, but the cursor didn't budge.

"Force quit."

He held down a couple of keys. The screen went blue, then black.

* * *

I called Spiner.

"Where the heck did you go?" she asked.

"System's down. Jeong and Martin are offended. Peggy and Liza are most likely packing their bags."

"I'll take Peggy."

After giving her the address, I hung up.

"Okay, Stephen. You and I get Liza."

We ran down the dimly lit stairs into the driving rain, then clambered into the car.

I drove fast as conditions permitted, which was about 20 miles per hour. I could barely see the EXIT sign for Interstate 78 to the Holland Tunnel.

Most of the streetlights and signals were out. Fewer than half the signs were lit.

"Good thing traffic's light," I said.

Stephen watched a Con Ed truck through his window. Two men in reflective yellow vests and blue hardhats inched their way toward a sparking power line on the pavement. "Except for these guys, we're the only ones dumb enough to be out on a night like this."

Without warning a semi roared past on our right, splashing the car with so much water I could barely see. When I honked my horn, it was a pathetic little beep.

I veered left, hoping to avoid another deluge. A guardrail loomed under one of the few working streetlights. The steering wheel vibrated in my grip.

Finally I stabilized and followed the taillights of what looked like a taxi in the distance. Nearing the tunnel, I slowed even more.

At least six inches of water covered the highway. A dozen cars or so were stalled, their engines flooded. Navigating to the tunnel entrance, I prayed the water wouldn't get any deeper.

I switched on the radio. Lightning flashed, followed by a burst of static.

While we waited I listened to the traffic report.

"Pretty grim," I said, and snapped it off. "If we can make it to Jersey City, we should be okay. God knows why the storm tapers off at the state line."

"Thought you'd be the first to know. He's your personal traffic reporter, isn't he?"

The taxi in front of us started to move. I looked ahead at the signs. "They used to take cash here."

"Not when you're going from New York to Jersey. Since nobody really *wants* to go there, it's free."

We entered the tunnel, whose white ceramic tiles were darker than usual. The right lane was blocked. Something resembling a backpack floated by.

Three policemen waved us past. Two more pushed a motorcycle out of the way, its frantic driver searching for something in the water.

I shivered. "Hate tunnels. Not many in Idaho, but when I was about ten, my mom and I were—"

There was a *crunch,* followed by a long scraping sound. "That's not us, is it?"

Stephen rolled down his window. Exhaust and gasoline fumes filled the air.

He looked down. "Afraid so."

At last, we emerged into half-light and saw the WELCOME TO NEW JERSEY sign. Everything was grayer than ever.

"Never could figure out why they call this the Garden State," I said.

Slowly we made our way to Liza's apartment building. I got the umbrella and hit the buzzer next to her mailbox. No one responded.

"Must not be working."

I got on the phone.

"This is Liza."

"Carolyn and Stephen here. Just wanted to wrap up our discussion."

She groaned. "Yeah, sure. Fine."

We climbed the stairs. I knocked on the door.

After 30 seconds of silence, I tried again. Nothing.

The door was unlocked. Stephen eased it open.

All was dark inside but for about two dozen candles, fragrant and undoubtedly homemade.

But their maker seemed to be gone.

CHAPTER 34

"MAYBE SHE WENT OUT THE WINDOW," STEPHEN whispered.

"On the third floor?" I asked.

We listened, but all we heard was wind.

Sitting on the couch, I took out my phone. Punching in Liza's number again, I got no answer.

"Wonder how Spiner's doing with Peggy?" I asked.

I tried the detective's number. She picked up but was hard to hear. I put her on speaker.

"Stuck in traffic. About halfway there. Streets are more or less flooded. Probably should be stopping and pushing cars onto the sidewalk or something. But let's face it—if you're dumb enough to drive your little Honda Civic into the Hudson River, you deserve what you get."

"We're at Liza's but she's not here. Was just a couple of minutes ago. Place looks like a Catholic church."

"Statues? What?"

"Candles all over. Reminds me of an altar."

"Don't know what to tell you. Search the place, maybe. Or just blow out the candles before it goes up in smoke. Or get yourselves out of there in case she's decided to take you on."

"A little dramatic, isn't it? She's got that bad arm. And there are two of us."

"Suit yourself."

* * *

I put the phone in my purse. "I say we just blow out *half* the candles. And take a look around."

Just in case, I took out my pepper spray.

Stephen counted the candles. He tried extinguishing one by licking his fingers and pinching the wick, but yelled and waved his hand to cool it.

"*Ow*," he said.

"You're no G. Gordon Liddy."

"Who?"

"Watergate. Mustache. Crazy."

He blew the rest out.

I pointed toward the kitchen. We tiptoed in.

He opened the refrigerator door.

"Can't you *ever* stop thinking about your stomach?" I asked.

"It's to give us some light. My phone's not enough. Also, I'm looking for an ice pack. Don't see any, though."

He paused. "Aha. What's this?" Lifting out a white chocolate sculpture shaped like the Arc de Triomphe, he proceeded to break off a cornerstone. "She'll never notice."

He put the rest of the landmark back and ate what he'd taken. The moans that ensued were disgusting.

"Need the biggest knife I can find," he said.

"Cut off any more, and she'll amputate your thumbs."

He rattled through the drawers. "Not for food."

"Plan to murder yourself?"

"Purely defensive."

Finally he pulled out a cleaver. "This should do."

"Remember, we're the good guys."

"Can't finish last. Not this time."

I checked the walk-in pantry. Liza wasn't there. Not that she'd fit between the Captain Crunch and the five-pound sack of Basmati rice.

We headed into the bedroom. There being no candles, we took out our smartphones and waved them around.

He got down on his knees and peered under the bed. "Not here."

I wondered if she owned a gun. Heart pounding, I opened the closet. Nothing.

"Bathroom," I whispered.

Stepping inside, I was momentarily blinded by my phone light's reflection in the mirror.

There was a rustling as the shower curtain was yanked open from the inside.

Liza stepped out of the tub with a pair of scissors and put her arm around my neck.

* * *

Doing my best not to run out of oxygen, I gaped. "Pinking shears?"

"Yeah."

I sucked in a deep breath. "When I was in grade school I used those on valentines. Not too sharp on the end. Unless you're planning to make me die of embarrassment by giving me a lousy haircut."

I tried to aim the pepper spray over my shoulder but couldn't.

Another lungful of air. "How can you do this with that awful case of carpal tunnel?"

"I manage. Now, here's what we're going to do. First, you drop the spray."

That was easy. Respiration was getting harder.

"We're going to leave and go to Peggy's place."

Stephen stepped into the bathroom. Eyes wide, he raised the cleaver.

"Oh, Stephen," she purred. "Really enjoyed your company. Doesn't look like it's going to work out, though."

"Liza, put those down," he said. "You don't want *two* murder charges."

"You got here late. Step one: Drop the cutlery so I don't have to turn your friend into a bloody valentine. Step two: We go visit Peggy Van Plugh."

He placed the cleaver on the toilet seat, which was covered by a light green knit cozy.

"Have to warn you," he said. "The roads are a mess. Traffic's terrible."

"That's why we need to start now."

CHAPTER 35

Sirens sounded in the distance. The rain had stopped, but side streets were clogged with stalled vehicles. When we reached the Holland Tunnel, I had to borrow Liza's E-ZPass to get through.

We parked near Peggy's apartment. Streetlamps and windows were starting to light up.

"Let's take a little walk," Liza said.

I could feel the tip of the shears like a sharpened Number Two Ticonderoga in my back. Looking around for Spiner's car, I didn't see it.

"You go first," Liza told Stephen. "So I can keep an eye on you."

"Wish I had that cleaver," he muttered.

"That's the bad attitude I'm talking about. Buzz us in."

Finding VAN PLUGH written precisely as an engraved brass nameplate, he pressed the button.

She elbowed past him. "We're here," she called.

"Come on up."

Another poke caught me near the seventh vertebra or so as Liza turned the doorknob. Her phone went off.

"Ignore it," she said.

We took the stairs to the second floor, passing three people in the hallway. They folded their umbrellas and shook their heads like canines at a Wag N' Wash.

"Last one on the left," she said. At the door she stretched around me and knocked.

For what seemed like half a minute I heard locks being turned and chains pulled out.

There stood Peggy, looking worried. "Anybody follow you?"

"Not that I know of," her partner said.

Sticking her head out, she surveyed the hall and motioned us inside.

* * *

The apartment looked like Trumbull's office, lined with bookshelves and pieces of replicated pre-Colombian art. I was surprised the latter weren't accompanied by museum-quality placards documenting their places and periods of origin.

My phone went off again.

Liza swore. "Can you tell who it is?"

"Looks like the detective."

"Good. We can wrap this up and move on. Go ahead, answer it."

I put it on speaker. "Almost there," Spiner said. "Fire engine's blocking the next intersection. I'll go the rest of the way on foot."

"We'll be waiting."

"Sit down," Peggy ordered.

Liza withdrew the scissors and rested them on her lap.

Peggy stepped sideways to her roll-top desk and

extracted a revolver. "For protection. Roger was always trying to get me to buy one. On my fifteenth anniversary he gave me this. Never thought I'd actually use it. But believe me, I know how."

I leaned forward. "Which of you did it first?"

Liza checked to make sure the gun was loaded. "Did what?"

"Stabbed Roger."

"What makes you think we did?"

"The eyewitness." I looked at Peggy. "Guess it has to be you. You came out with the hats before five. And Liza, you went in a few minutes later with the bag."

Peggy snapped the cylinder shut. "So what? Hats, bags—hardly murder weapons."

"Gina Casebeer heard at least one person enter and leave Roger's office just before she passed out."

Taking the scissors, Liza snipped a stray thread from the sofa pillow. "Good for her. Doesn't know whether she's coming or going. And whose prints are on the knife? Hers."

I rubbed the stinging spot on my back. "All you needed to do was wrap her fingers around it while she was out."

The intercom razzed. Peggy sauntered over and buzzed back.

"Detective Spiner, NYPD. I'm here about—"

"I know. Come on up."

Peggy put the gun in her pocket.

Liza hid the scissors in her purse.

"Surprised you two could work together," I said. "Of course, you did have an enemy in common."

"Know something?" Liza asked. "You talk too much."

I ignored her. "So what's the end game here? You shoot us? Cut us up? Kill a police officer?"

They looked at each other and shook their heads.

"We've got no evidence to hide," Peggy said. "And what crime have we committed? You can't prove you didn't come here of your own free will. Your case against us is circumstantial. The one against Gina is cut and dried."

"Open and shut," Liza added. "We may not be lawyers, but we know some pretty good ones."

There was a rap at the door. Peggy opened it.

There stood Spiner, displaying her badge. "Peggy Maria Van Plugh?"

"That's me."

The detective slid past her. "Liza Cicely Boxer?"

"We've met."

"You're both under arrest."

* * *

Peggy's smug expression started to melt. "On what charge?"

"The murder of Roger Trumbull."

Peggy's hand moved toward her pocket.

Liza reached for her purse.

I nodded at Peggy. "She's got a gun."

Stephen pointed at Liza. "Scissors at two o'clock."

Spiner drew her weapon.

Peggy took aim. Jumping up, I tried to wrestle away her revolver.

"For God's sake, get out of the way!" the detective yelled.

Stephen dashed toward Liza, grabbed her arm, and squeezed the wrist brace with both hands. The scissors dropped to the floor.

Spiner fired.

With a shriek Peggy bent over. The gun fell from her grip. With her right hand she covered her left thigh.

Spiner took one pair of handcuffs from her long leather jacket and tossed another to Stephen.

"You know how these work?" she asked.

"Of course."

She snapped the shackles on Peggy's wrists.

Trying to do the same, Stephen pinched two fingers in the process. He started sucking on them.

I took the cuffs and put them on Peggy. A red stain slowly soaked through her jeans.

Spiner got on her phone. "I need backup."

* * *

Next morning we visited Gina in jail. She looked worse than ever.

We told her what had happened.

She closed her eyes. "Thank God, or whoever."

Stephen knocked on the glass and showed her his bandaged fingers. "She resisted arrest."

"So sorry," she said, but didn't look it.

I smiled. "Your lawyer says you should be out by noon."

"They all say that."

"No, really. It's over. I remember how I felt when you got *me* out. When you're ready, we should celebrate."

"I can't get the last month of my life back."

"But you can get back to work. Comfier chairs, and the food's better."

"And you can sleep all you want," Stephen added.

Gina frowned and folded her arms across her chest.

He flinched. "Oh, the narcolepsy thing. My bad."

I stood up. "Call us when they let you out. We'll give you a ride anywhere you want to go."

"I'll be ready."

I blew her a kiss.

We found our way to the visitors' lot. "Wonder where Peggy and Liza will do their time?" I asked. "Assuming they don't get away with murder."

"They won't," Stephen said. "Good lawyer. The old guy's testimony."

He paused. "I know the perfect place. Ever see *Escape from Alcatraz?*" Clint Eastwood and Patrick McGoohan. McGoohan's the warden."

"Alcatraz is closed."

"Yeah, but he was so sadistic. And Clint Eastwood drove him crazy."

"Speaking of which, we'll have to tell Hunter."

I was about to call him when my phone rang. It was Gina.

"They're processing me. I should be done in about fifteen minutes." I could tell she was grinning.

"Meet us at the gate," I said. "Preferably outside."

EPILOGUE

Four months later Gina was promoted to Senior Director of the Legal Department. Her neurologist adjusted her medication so she could sleep only when she wanted to—mainly when Hunter was talking.

Peggy and Liza were convicted and sentenced to life in prison with no possibility of parole. Their unsuccessful appeal was filed by Alexander Washington, who took their case after being injured in a kayaking accident and losing the ability to snap his suspenders.

Six months later Martin Curry passed away, leaving his collection of jokes and rubber novelties to Stephen, who gave them to a rabbi who used them to take third place on *America's Got Talent*.

Elaine Jeong disappeared, then returned as Lane Chung, a transgendered bodybuilder who was hired by the New York City Mayor's Office to teach bureaucrats how to dance around regulations regarding inappropriate touching.

Jordan Spiner quit the force and became a fashion

designer known primarily for her work in leather, especially a *Matrix* line of wallets and key chains.

Kenny Humboldt went on to acting school. He did mostly commercials, but successfully auditioned for the Matthew McConaughey role in *Sahara Two: Sunburn and Sand*. The film was never made, and he retired early to live on a houseboat.

Lee Kirby, the guard with the orange glasses, moved up the ladder to sentinel at the headquarters of Marvel Comics.

Kathleen Rosenthal starred in a one-woman show based on her book. Pendleton House got 40 percent for performance rights, which probably paid for Hunter's new office golf course.

Joey moved to some tropical island, or so it was rumored. His band broke up and all those leftover CDs were donated to the New York School for the Deaf, which rejected them.

As for me, I've permanently sworn off dating lawyers, especially ones who are dead.

IF YOU LIKED THIS, YOU MAY ENJOY: ADRENOCHROME

BY JOHN THEO JR.

A contemporary, Christian mystery pulled straight from today's headlines.

Cattle farmer, and part time Private Investigator, Brandon Hall is still recovering from the loss of his herd when government agent Roger Drake shows up with a side job. Billionaire playboy Geoffrey Cavendish, recently arrested for sex trafficking, is found dead in prison of an apparent suicide.

Brandon is tasked with retrieving Cavendish's sole business partner, Gabrielle Maxine Walters, and escort her to Washington DC where she has agreed to exchange information for clemency. What promises to be a simple babysitting job turns out to be far more dangerous than Brandon ever expected.

Alone, and on the run, Brandon must protect Gabrielle Walters at all costs and deliver her safely to the Attorney General while being pursued by treasonous deep-state cells within the government.

**As with all of John Theo Jr.'s novels, Adrenochrome is devoid of foul language, and gratuitous sex scenes, but does contain tough subject matter.*

OUT NOW ON AMAZON

IF YOU LIKED THIS, YOU MAY ENJOY
ADRENOCHROME
BY JOHN [illegible]

A contemporary Christian mystery pulled straight from today's headlines.

[illegible]

ABOUT THE AUTHOR

John Duckworth is a novelist, editor, playwright, scriptwriter, cartoonist, and father of twins. After earning his bachelor's degree at Linfield College, he spent 35 years in the publishing industry as a curmudgeonly editor, product developer, and author, working with people like Ken Blanchard, Dr. Kevin Leman, Richard Foster, and Calvin Miller, producers like VeggieTales, organizations like Focus on the Family and companies like Random House, Thomas Nelson, NavPress, Group Publishing, Zondervan and Rainfall Toys.

His works include *Joan 'n' the Whale, Just for a Moment I Saw the Light,* four collections of short plays, a ton of curriculum, at least 90 articles and short stories and three videos about a giant chipmunk puppet. He also contributed chapters to several trade books, edited scores of nonfiction and fiction titles, wrote animation and live action scripts for a major video series, several ounces of online content, and co-directed a traveling drama troupe called the Jericho Roadshow. On the radio he's done voice-over work for the popular *Adventures in Odyssey* program and wrote, directed, and performed in *The Semi-Amusing Half-Hour Comedy Show.*

After producing nearly 250 issues of weekly publications *Power for Living* and *FreeWay,* he created seven multi-volume series of youth ministry resources. He's edited or rewritten hundreds of books, articles, and lesson plans.

John's hobbies include figuring out how to promote himself while pretending to be humble, reading stories to children in the hospital, holding tiny babies in the neonatal intensive care unit, and feeding the cat. He and his lovely wife, Liz, live in Colorado Springs.

www.ingramcontent.com/pod-product-compliance
Lightning Source LLC
LaVergne TN
LVHW030920080826
845145LV00013B/2975

* 9 7 8 1 6 4 7 3 4 5 3 9 6 *